To: Melissa V"

Always follow your creative dreams!

2013

D1293300

MELISSA M. WILLIAMS

CRAZY DAYS OF 5TH GRADE

An Iggy the Iguana Book

ILLUSTRATED BY
KELLEY STENGELE

LongTale®
PUBLISHING

To Josh

1974 - 2011

Contents

1
Nothing's the Same

Iggy watched Mr. Gruff eat the sports section of the *Houston Chronicle* as he waited anxiously for class to begin. The goat literally scarfed down each page without even looking at the score reports. Iggy assumed that meant he wasn't an Astros' fan. But then again, he had heard rumors that goats eat pretty much *everything*.

Iggy slumped down in his chair and sighed. The iguana wasn't looking forward to being in Mr. Gruff's class. Everyone at school knew he was the meanest teacher at Memorial Elementary, not to mention the oldest.

Mr. Gruff looked up from his paper and glared at the

kid sitting to Iggy's left. Out of the corner of his eye, Iggy spotted a Texas Rattler. Now it made sense why he kept hearing a rattling noise. Oddly enough, the sound coming from the rattlesnake reminded Iggy of the ocean, which of course reminded him of his best friend, Snap Shell. Iggy had only been back from his trip to Turtle Town, California for a few days, and he already missed the turtle.

Liz the lizard passed by his desk on her way to the pencil sharpener. Iggy hadn't seen Liz since the All-Star baseball tournament last summer. She looked a lot taller than what he remembered. He wondered if Liz could fulfill the role of his new best friend.

Iggy looked over at Kit Kat and Buddy, his baseball pals. They were busy making paper airplanes and throwing them across the room every time Mr. Gruff looked down at his half chewed newspaper. Marc sat next to Iggy, but he didn't talk much.

Cooper the chameleon was camouflaged in the corner, well somewhat. He was making a spinner out of notebook paper. The only thing missing was Snap.

The ring of the school bell shot the iguana out of his thoughts and Mr. Gruff out of his seat. The morning announcements began, followed immediately by the Pledge of Allegiance. Everyone in the class put their hand over their heart and Sid, the new snake, put his rattle over his. Iggy noticed Marc wasn't saying anything, probably because this was his first year at an American school.

A moment of silence followed, and Mr. Gruff trotted to the front of the room. He neighed to quiet the class down and said, "We will start the morning with introductions." He paused and pointed to the back of the room at Cooper, who was now messing with the classroom fossil collection. "You in the back, take your seat."

The chameleon froze and his upper body took on the shade of the blue bulletin board behind him, leaving his lower half completely exposed and visible. He whispered to Kit Kat, "Do you think he can still see me?"

Kit Kat looked around the room with a big grin on his face and said, "Who said that?"

"Yes I *can* still see you! SIT DOWN!" Mr. Gruff continued on, "Everyone will come up to the front of class and tell us one thing and *only* one thing about yourself. I'll start. Gregory Gruff, but you will call me Mr. Gruff. I've been teaching for thirty years, and I enjoy playing in the archery games. Next."

Kit Kat raised his paw.

"You. Big cat. You're next," Mr. Gruff said, looking over his circular spectacles to get a better look at who would be his first volunteer.

"I was going to tell you that was more than one thing." Kit Kat leaned back, almost tipping over his chair.

"Enough! All chair legs on the ground. Come to the front of the class, drop and give me twenty."

"Twenty? Like twenty things about myself?" Kit Kat asked.

"No smart cat. Twenty push-ups." Mr. Gruff pointed to the ground next to his hooves. "And take off that ball cap!"

"Seriously?" Kit Kat asked as his chair slammed to the ground.

A few animals giggled, but Mr. Gruff did not have a sense of humor.

Kit Kat took off his cap, got out of his seat and managed to do two push-ups, hoping to get a few more laughs from his audience no doubt.

The goat shook his head in disgust. "Your homework will be to start doing twenty push-ups at home every day. I do not tolerate laziness!" Mr. Gruff said and went on about how physical fitness is the number one indicator of strength and success.

Once Kit Kat dusted off his furry knees, he began, "My name is Kit Kat Kay Kat. That's cat with a K, and I enjoy a good, mouth-watering twinkie." The cat bowed and walked back to his seat.

Iggy watched Mr. Gruff shake his head and point at Sid next. The sound coming from Sid's rattle took on a new pitch as he slithered up to the front.

"The name'ssssss Sssssssid." His lip quivered as he forced a smile and adjusted his bow tie using the tip of his rattle. "I transssssssferred from an all ssssssnake academy in Dallassssss, Texassssss," Sid said and slithered quickly back to his seat and coiled up in his chair.

By the time it was Iggy's turn, his green scales had taken on a nervous red tint. He never really liked public speaking. Plus he couldn't decide whether to talk about his trip to California to visit his best friend or his arm injury from last summer. Once he got to the front of the room and turned to face his audience, all of his ideas went out the window and he said, "I would like to be a baseball coach when I grow up." He looked over at Liz sitting across the room who was smiling at him. "Oh. And my name is Iggy Green." He darted back to his seat, his tail knocking over a pencil box sitting on the desk behind him.

"Excuse you!" The girl behind him said with an attitude. Iggy realized he didn't recognize the voice. He reached down quickly to grab the box and saw that it was covered in rhinestones. He inspected it for a brief second and turned to find a little green iguana tapping her foot at him.

"Can I have my makeup case back?" she sighed and rolled her eyes.

"Your makeup case?" Iggy questioned looking down at the pencil box in his hand. "Oh, this?"

"Duh!" She grabbed it from his hand, and Iggy immediately sat down.

Samantha the skunk was already at the front of the room when Iggy regained his composure. Samantha opened her mouth, but nothing came out.

"Go on." Mr. Gruff motioned with his hoof for her to continue.

7

A few of the animals started to giggle. Iggy detected a strange aroma that he usually only smelled on road trips. Samantha backed up, and that's when Kit Kat yelled, "Stink Bomb!"

Everyone in the class held their noses and took cover, knowing that Samantha accidently sprayed every time she got nervous, angry or excited.

"Quiet! Everyone back in your chairs." Mr. Gruff coughed, barely getting the words out as he waved his hand in front of him to move the musk along. He allowed Samantha to excuse herself and covered his nose for a brief second while catching his breath.

Iggy could hear Kit Kat gagging obnoxiously in the back of the room while the rest of the class tried to hold their noses and not breathe in the air. Iggy figured she must have been more nervous than he for that much odor to come out of the little skunk.

Once the class settled down, Marc was next. Marc was very tiny for a fifth grader, but he was also a mouse. He wore an interesting looking beret on his head and when he spoke everyone got quiet. Marc's Spanish accent and deep voice echoed. "My *nombre* is Marcus Mouse."

Kit Kat interrupted, "Why does he get to wear a hat in class?"

"That does not concern you. Please continue Marc," Mr. Gruff said encouragingly.

"*Yo soy* from Madrid," the mouse said. Every once in a while Marc mixed Spanish and English together in the same sentence, which helped Iggy learn a few new words in Spanish.

Mr. Gruff made a note on his attendance sheet and walked back to his desk.

Liz the lizard talked about softball during her introduction. Buddy the bullfrog talked about his summer trip to New York to see his family. Cooper the chameleon didn't really have much to say at all.

Just when the introductions were about to put Iggy to sleep, Isabella, the little green iguana who sat behind him, stood up and strutted to the front of the class. Cooper let out a whistle, and Iggy perked up. On her way to the front, she stopped by Mr. Gruff's desk to hand him a red soda can, which he gratefully accepted and stuffed down his throat.

"Suck up," Kit Kat muttered under his breath.

Isabella looked older than all the other girls in class. She had on a fancy blue dress, and Iggy could tell she was even wearing makeup. Isabella began with her favorite places to go shopping which included L.A., Paris and New York City. She went on and on for what seemed like twenty minutes with facts about herself. "I'm half Portuguese and half French. I've won every spelling bee since I was in the first grade. Oh, and I'm rich."

Iggy thought that seemed like a good stopping point, but Mr. Gruff let her continue.

Once Isabella finally concluded her self-proclaimed autobiography, she passed by Iggy to get to her desk. She smelled like the perfume inside Iggy's mom's magazines. He watched her fix her dress just before she sat down, and that's when Kit Kat mimicked a sound that should only be heard inside the bathroom. The class burst into an uproar of laughter. Isabella pursed her lips and glared at the cat.

"Enough!" Mr. Gruff slammed his hoof on the desk. He grabbed a stack of papers and walked directly up to Iggy. "Please pass these out to each student."

Iggy agreed without saying a word.

Kit Kat raised his paw.

"What is it?" Mr. Gruff looked like he wanted to head-butt Kit Kat in the face.

"Can I sharpen my pencil?"

"No!"

Cooper raised his hand.

"What?" the goat huffed.

"Can I use the bathroom?"

"Do I look like a substitute teacher to you? Enough with the questions and trickery. Hold it!"

Mr. Gruff eyed Iggy and waited for him to get back in his seat. "These are review packets examining your knowledge of social studies, reading and science from last year. Please take the morning to read over the material."

Iggy looked down at his first story. It was titled, *The Enslavement of Lions and Gorillas in the early 1900s.*

11

Boring, he thought to himself. He didn't remember having to learn about this topic in fourth grade. It was nearly impossible for him to read without drifting off into a daydream about a cartoon he had once seen where a lion cub had to save his land after his father died. Too bad they weren't watching a movie about this stuff. Iggy flipped through the packet, shocked to find there was not one picture in the entire thing.

Unfortunately Iggy's opinion didn't matter, because the next thing Mr. Gruff put on his desk was a pop quiz. Iggy began to panic. He didn't know they would be quizzed on this stuff. It was only the first day of school.

"You have forty minutes before lunch to complete your quiz. You may use your packets. Write in complete sentences only. And no cheating!" the goat bleated.

Cooper raised his hand, and Mr. Gruff whipped around. "Now what?"

"There's no multiple choice?" the chameleon asked.

"Multiple choice?" the goat cross-examined.

"Yeah, you know, the ones that you bubble in," Kit Kat said without raising his paw.

"Do I look like some new age teacher to you?" the goat questioned.

Iggy thought Mr. Gruff looked more like a fossil.

"Everyone listen up. You are in Mr. Gruff's class now," he threw his hooves up in air quotes and continued, "and we will not be *bubbling in* answers. We will be writing essays and drawing conclusions. Intelligence should not be measured by chance but by true knowledge of subject matter. One day you will appreciate my methods."

The class didn't say a word.

"Begin your essays ... NOW!" the goat commanded.

Essays? Iggy thought. He hadn't even gotten to the science section yet. Iggy looked around the room to see if anyone else was as shocked as he.

"Iggy," Mr. Gruff said.

Iggy jumped. "Yes?"

"No cheating."

"I wasn't sir."

"And no talking."

Iggy bit his lip. Mr. Gruff was even worse than he

expected. He flipped back through his packet, but unfortunately he needed to read the whole thing over again in order to compare the lions and gorillas.

At twelve o'clock sharp, Mr. Gruff ordered the class to put down their pencils. Iggy scrambled to finish his last sentence.

"I said pencils down Iggy!" The goat commanded, while standing over him. He grabbed Iggy's paper and told everyone to line up for lunch. Iggy sighed, knowing that he *for sure* failed his first quiz.

After marching, *literally*, in a perfectly straight line, the animals scrambled apart once they hit the cafeteria. Iggy followed his friends to the fifth grade table and pulled out his sandwich. A fly settled in for a landing on his bread at the same time a bright pink tongue shot across the table.

"Score!" Buddy yelled and sat down next to Kit Kat. "That fly was about to eat Iggy's sandwich!" the frog said and pulled out a bag of his own dried flies.

"Ewww! What are those?" Isabella walked up with Liz and pointed at Buddy's bag.

"A delicacy. Here try one!" Buddy handed Isabella a cracker garnished with a fly.

"That is so disgusting!" Isabella groaned.

"Not as bad as what Old Gruff eats!" Cooper said and sat down next to Isabella. "Did you see him inhale that can Isabella gave him?"

"Yeah. I wonder if I bring him a can of worms, if he'll eat that tomorrow," Kit Kat laughed.

"Go for it," Cooper said.

"I might as well, he already doesn't like me," the cat said, stuffing a huge bite of pineapple pizza in his mouth.

"He doesn't like me either," Iggy said.

"He's only being strict because it's the first day of school. You will all be fine." Liz reassured the boys, then changed the subject. "Iggy, didn't you go to California last week to see Snap?"

"Yeah. I got back a few days ago after his competition," the iguana said taking a bite of his sandwich.

"Competition? What kind of competition?" Buddy looked up from his flies.

"Surfing."

"Snap can surf?" Liz asked and spotted the necklace around Iggy's neck. "Did he give you his favorite necklace too?"

"Oh this?" Iggy held up the puka shell necklace. "No, he took me down to a shell stand to get one of my own," Iggy said and kept on. "All the beach animals wear these things. He's got a bunch of new friends too. Mostly sea turtles."

"So is he any good?" Buddy asked.

"He's like a pro!"

"No way!" the frog exclaimed.

Everyone seemed intrigued and reminisced about all of the fun times they had with the box shell turtle, everyone except Isabella.

She instantly spoke up again. "My dad has a beach house in Malibu. We fly to California every summer to stay with my Tia Antoinette."

"What's a tia?" Cooper asked.

Marc answered for her. "It's Spanish for aunt."

"I like ants." Cooper grinned and kept staring at Isabella.

16

Isabella rolled her eyes and kept on talking. "She like owns this amazing dress shop in La Jolla. I get all of my dresses and purses there." Isabella held up her designer purse. Iggy watched Liz pretend to be interested, or at least he figured she was only pretending. Liz didn't care about purses and dresses. She liked sports. *Right?*

Once lunch was over, a small honey badger blew a whistle and yelled for everyone to line up.

"Looks like we've got a new lunch lady," Iggy said to Buddy.

"That's a lady?" Buddy asked.

"She's wearing a dress," Iggy said.

"You know what they say about badgers ..." Marc spoke up again.

"No, what?" Iggy looked down at the little mouse.

"Vicious," Marc said. "Don't mess with them."

Iggy watched the lunch lady yank Digger Dog by his collar and tell him to throw away his trash.

"I'll keep that in mind. It looks like Digger got stuck with sweeping the lunchroom floor," Iggy said.

Once the class met Mrs. Buff at the door, they headed

to the field for recess with the other fifth grade class. Mrs. Buff would be Iggy's computer teacher, which was the only good news for the day as far as he was concerned. The old terrier was still drinking from her usual mug of coffee like last year. The smell of her coffee and dog breath was surprisingly comforting, and Iggy decided he would take it over Mr. Gruff's voice any day.

"Soccer! I'm a team captain!" Cooper called out once they reached the field.

"I'm on Iggy's team then," Buddy said.

Iggy turned around to ask Liz to be on his team, but he spotted her walking over by the gate with Isabella. "Liz!" he shouted. She just waved.

"Come on Iggy! Pick a boy," Cooper said and smirked. "Liz has a new friend."

Iggy looked back at Liz one more time. She loved sports, but talking to Isabella seemed more important at the moment, so Iggy picked Marc.

Kit Kat and Buddy took their positions as goalies on opposite sides of the field, and the others assumed their positions as well. Due to Marc's moves and swiftness, he scored on Kit Kat every time he got the ball and won the game.

"That cheese brain is fast!" Kit Kat meowed as they headed back inside.

"No, you're just slow!" Cooper yelled at his teammate.

Iggy ignored the boys' comments and walked inside with Marc. At the water fountain Iggy noticed Marc was still breathing pretty hard from his win.

"You doing okay?" Iggy asked the mouse.

"*Si,*" Marc said and followed Iggy to computer class.

Inside the computer lab, Liz was *still* chatting with Isabella and didn't even bother congratulating Iggy and his team on their win, which wasn't like her at all.

"What in the world could they still be talking about?" Iggy asked Marc.

"Gossip?" Marc suggested.

"Of course," Iggy said.

At the end of the day, Iggy couldn't get to his locker fast enough once the bell rang. He collected everything he needed for homework, which was practically his entire locker thanks to Mr. Gruff. He zipped up his backpack and walked over to Liz to see if she wanted a ride home from school.

"Thanks Iggy, but I'm going over to Isabella's house today," she replied.

Isabella handed Liz a pink cell phone, which was also covered in rhinestones, from her purse so she could call her mom. The prissy iguana looked at Iggy, rolled her eyes and said, "Oh, it's you." She linked arms with Liz to pull her along.

Liz turned around once they got halfway down the hall. "Bye Iggy!"

"See ya," Iggy sighed. It looked like Liz wouldn't be in line for his new best friend this year.

2
The Teacher Ate
My Homework!

Iggy followed slowly behind the girls who were giggling about some dumb singer from Isabella's magazine. Thankfully he spotted his little sister as soon as he got outside. Now that Molly was in grade school and attending Memorial Elementary, it was Iggy's responsibility to keep up with her, especially on the days they had to walk home. Today Mrs. Green picked them both up so Molly could make it to dance class on time.

When Iggy saw his mom's car, he waved for Molly to come over, but she continued talking to her best friend, Little Bit the turtle.

"Molly!" Iggy yelled from across the school lawn.

Molly turned back and put her hands on her hips. "I'm trying to say bye to Miss Jay!" she said and hop scotched over to her teacher. Iggy looked at his mom who was making the *hurry up* face through the car window. Iggy pointed at his sister taking her dear old time.

Once Molly was finished with her teacher, she skipped past Iggy intentionally but waited for him to open the car door for her. Iggy opened the back door, and she jumped in next to an egg wrapped in a felt blanket, sitting in a car seat. Over the summer, Mrs. Green had laid an egg, and it was expected to hatch any day now.

"Hey Mom." Iggy sat down in the front seat and buckled his seat belt.

"Hi kids. How was your first day at school?"

Molly jumped at the chance to talk. "Fabulous! I love first grade!"

"Was that blue jay you were hugging your teacher?" Mrs. Green asked.

"Yes! Isn't she gorgeous?"

"Yes dear. You finally got a bird for a teacher like you've always wanted." Mrs. Green smiled and started driving toward the dance studio. "What about you Iggy?"

"I have a goat," Iggy answered.

"I have a goat in my class too!" Molly chimed in. "Her name's Billie!"

"Cool," Iggy said unenthusiastically.

"Does she have horns?" Molly inquired.

"Yes Molly. Two of them. And it's a he."

Mrs. Green continued with the questions. "Did you have a nice time with your classmates Iggy?"

"It was okay. The whole baseball team is practically in my class this year."

"The whole baseball team! Even Cooper?" Mrs. Green asked.

"Yeah, Cooper too. Why?"

"I don't know about that Cooper kid. I get a bad feeling about him."

"Mom, everything's cool. Besides he's our neighbor now."

"Exactly. I've been keeping an eye on him."

"Mom!" Molly screamed.

"What's the matter Molly?!" Mrs. Green shouted and slammed on the brakes.

"The egg is touching me!"

Iggy turned around to find that Molly was practically sitting in the egg's chair. "Then scoot over Molly. You could've caused an accident!" Iggy shook his head. Molly was constantly blaming the egg for everything ... from her bad moods, to her not being able to fall asleep at night and her itchy skin. Molly was such a drama queen. Iggy was hoping when the egg hatched it would be a boy.

◆　◆　◆

Later that evening, as Iggy was doing his social studies homework, he turned on his laptop to get on-line. He saw that Snap Shell was also on-line and sent him a message. He *had* to tell Snap about his horrible first day of school.

The turtle instantly responded with a *what's up brah?!* Iggy started to feel better after venting to Snap, until

Snap told him that he tested out of fifth grade and got moved into sixth grade at Cardiff School by the Sea.

Iggy almost fell out of his chair. *What? Are you serious?* Iggy typed.

Totally! Snap typed back.

Iggy sighed and typed, *I'm really excited for you,* trying his best to be genuinely happy for the turtle, but in reality he felt awful. Here his best friend got bumped up a level, and he couldn't even finish a review quiz on the first day of school.

Snap told Iggy to hang in there and reassured him that the goat wasn't out to get him. Easy for him to say, Snap probably had a cool turtle teacher who let them surf on their lunch breaks. Snap logged off to go surf with his new friends, and Iggy decided to look up airline tickets to California while he was still on-line.

After finally completing all of his homework, Iggy figured he should write down the Pledge of Allegiance for Marc to help him memorize it. He thought Marc would make a good best friend, so he should start looking out for him.

Iggy crawled into bed exhausted from the day. He fell asleep in the middle of praying, "And please, please let the egg be a b..."

The following morning Iggy spent a little extra time in the bathroom adding mousse to his spikes. He pulled out a little vile of cologne that he got from his older cousin, Dragon D, and dabbed a few drops on his neck. After taking one last look in the mirror, he headed downstairs to the kitchen for breakfast.

"You smell nice honey. Who are you trying to impress at school?" his mom asked and set a bowl of oatmeal and strawberries on the table for him.

"No one mom! Why do you say things like that?" Iggy dropped down on the kitchen floor to do a few push-ups in case Mr. Gruff asked.

Mr. Green walked into the kitchen with his gym bag. "Morning Champ! Doing some training?"

"Nah, just homework. The story of my life," Iggy said.

"I like it! Well, you better get your sister, or the two of you are going to be late," his father suggested.

Iggy ate his oatmeal quickly and went back upstairs

and into his sister's room. Her bed was made, and the room was empty, except for Molly's pet dragonfly that was flying around like a crazy bug. He went to the next best place to find Molly, the nursery. Sure enough Molly was sitting criss-crossed in front of the crib, staring at the egg.

"Molly, we're leaving. Get your stuff," Iggy said.

"Shhhh. It's trying to tell me something." Molly scooted up closer to the egg.

"Did you draw a mouth on the egg this time?"

"No." She smirked innocently.

"Come on or we're going to be late."

"Fine!" Molly got up and sprinted past her big brother.

"And eggs don't talk," Iggy yelled after her. The older the egg got, the more obsessed Molly became with it. She had already made a list of names for when it hatched, which included Bubbles, Pixie and Pinkie. And the last time Iggy caught her in the nursery, she was crying and said the egg was staring at her. That was probably because Molly had drawn eyes on the egg with her watercolors.

Once Iggy got downstairs, his mom kissed him and his sister good-bye and wished them a great day at school. The word, *school*, made Iggy cringe and picture Mr. Gruff's mean old face.

On the walk to school, Iggy noticed Molly was carrying a tiny bag. "What's that?"

"Birdseed for Miss Jay of course," she said.

Iggy laughed thinking maybe he should have brought a can to get on his teacher's good side.

After dropping off Molly at Miss Jay's room, he walked down the hall and into his class. He turned in his homework and put the Pledge he wrote for Marc on the mouse's desk. As he started on his morning assignment, he watched his classmates walk inside. Liz and Isabella came through the door together, both wearing purple dresses and matching bracelets. That was the first time Iggy had ever seen Liz wear a dress. Liz smiled and awkwardly sat down trying to make sure all sides of her dress were down.

Iggy laughed to himself.

"What?" Liz asked.

He didn't realize she heard him. "Oh nothing. You look nice," Iggy said.

"Did you put mousse on your spikes?" she asked.

He instantly blushed. The bell rang and Mr. Gruff took roll call as the morning announcements came over the loud speaker. Everyone was present, except for Marc, so Iggy grabbed the paper off Marc's desk when the class stood up for the Pledge.

Once the announcements were finished, the class continued on their morning work until Mr. Gruff started a lesson on democracy. He went on and on with so many details and examples, which Iggy was sure he would never need to know. The goat's mouth was moving, but

Iggy completely stopped listening and watched Cooper make a fortune teller out of paper.

"Iggy!" Mr. Gruff said.

Iggy perked up.

"Eyes on me," the goat said as he walked over to Cooper and grabbed the paper toy out of his hand. Mr. Gruff ended the lesson and told the class to answer the questions at the end of the chapter.

Iggy read question one, but it didn't make sense to him how he was supposed to critically examine the benefits of a republic as opposed to a direct democracy. He thought they both sounded good. Re-reading the paragraph about it in his social studies book didn't help and neither did Cooper's pencil tapping. He couldn't just sit there all day, so he got up to see if Mr. Gruff would help him.

Mr. Gruff was munching on a piece of notebook paper and actually reading the *Wall Street Journal*. Iggy approached his desk and did a double take. The paper Mr. Gruff had in his mouth had *Iggy's* name on it.

"Um, Mr. Gruff?"

The goat looked up. "What is it Iggy?"

"Well, sir. I first had a question about number one, but I couldn't help notice ..." Iggy paused and squinted making sure it really was *his* paper.

"Come out with it," Mr. Gruff huffed.

"Are you eating my homework?"

Mr. Gruff dropped the paper in his mouth. "This? Why, yes, this is yours. Garbage Iggy! I eat garbage!"

"But I answered every question sir."

"You're a daydreamer Iggy. I know you can do better."

"Huh?" Iggy stood there dumbfounded, wondering how his teacher knew he liked to daydream.

Mr. Gruff got up from his chair and grabbed a stack of papers off the top tray. "Here pass these back to their proper owners." He handed the papers to Iggy and walked to the front of the class again.

"Students. Iggy will be passing back your homework. If you don't receive anything back, that means ... I ate it! I eat sub-standard homework. Read the questions thoroughly and answer *every* part. You will re-do your homework until it is right! You've had enough time to waste on video games and TV this summer."

Mr. Gruff paused for a moment and examined the room. "And don't think I don't know which one of you didn't even bother to turn in your homework." He looked directly at Kit Kat whose head was looking down in his lap. Mr. Gruff nonchalantly walked up to the cat and grabbed Kit Kat's cell phone out of his paw. "Texting huh?" Mr. Gruff walked back to his desk and dropped the cell phone into his drawer.

"Grumpy goat," Kit Kat mumbled under his breath.

"What did you say to me?" The goat turned around. Kit Kat didn't say a word.

"Someone better tell me what was said, or we will all do push-ups at recess."

"I'll tell you!" Isabella blurted out. "He said *grumpy goat.*"

"Thank you Isabella. Kit Kat ... push-ups at recess for a week."

"What? That's my *me* time!"

"And now it's my time," Mr. Gruff said.

After Iggy passed back papers to only half of his class, Mr. Gruff told the class to pick a partner to finish the rest of their assignment.

Sid slithered over to Iggy and asked if they could be partners. Relieved, Iggy gladly accepted the invitation and immediately asked Sid if he understood number one. Sid was already on question seven and was thrilled to be of service.

Later that afternoon, Iggy was surprised to see his father in the carpool lane. When Iggy got in the car, his dad threw him his glove and ball cap.

"Want to head to the field to throw around the ball?" Iggy's dad asked excitedly.

"Really?" Iggy saw that Molly was already in the backseat with her best friend Little Bit, and they were both holding pom poms. Iggy assumed that meant they were coming along to the field too.

"Cool. I've got my lucky ball in my backpack," Iggy said. "Anything to get out of here."

"What's the problem Champ?" his dad asked. "How was school?"

"Besides the fact that my teacher ate my homework, pretty awesome," he said sarcastically.

"Why would your teacher eat your homework?"

"Because he said it was garbage."

"Garbage? Isn't that a little harsh?" Mr. Green asked.

"That's Mr. Gruff Dad! He is a mean, grumpy demanding goat!"

"Billie ate my eraser on the playground today!" Molly butted in, and Little Bit giggled.

"Son, I remember fifth grade being a big year for me when I was your age. It does seem hard, but it'll get better. It's all a part of growing up."

Didn't Mr. Green hear that Iggy's teacher *ate*, not *lost*, but ate his homework? If this was what growing up was all about, he would rather just stay a kid.

Mr. Green was about to give a few more words of advice when his cell phone rang. Iggy looked over and saw it was his mom calling.

"What?!" Mr. Green yelled into the phone. "I'm on my way! We're down the street!" Mr. Green hung up the phone and looked at his son. "Iggy, you are the big brother to ..." Iggy's heart stopped, hoping to hear the word boy.

"A little girl!" Mr. Green exclaimed.

Iggy's heart sank. This day was just getting better and better. *NOT*!

"Molly you too," their father said.

Molly squealed, "Me? The egg. I'm not a big brother!"

"He meant sister," Iggy grumbled.

"But I don't want to be a big anything. I like being small!"

Iggy figured Molly wanted the egg to stay an egg forever. He was really hoping for a boy, considering another little *Molly* running around would be two too many. "Really Dad? A girl?" Iggy looked at his father.

Mr. Green patted Iggy on his knee and asked him to call Little Bit's mom to let her know they wouldn't be stopping by the field anymore.

Once they dropped off Little Bit at her house, the iguanas rushed home and everyone ran into the nursery to find Mrs. Green in her chair, rocking the new baby iguana to sleep.

Molly got up in her new baby sister's face to inspect. "It looks like an alien."

Mr. Green picked up Molly and leaned down to kiss

his wife and new daughter on the forehead. She lay sound asleep in her mother's arms.

"That's exactly what you looked like when you were born Molly," Iggy said.

"Whatever! What should I name her?" Molly asked her father.

"We already have a name dear." Her mother smiled down at the baby and said, "Lily."

"Oh, I like that name. It's like a flower. I could call her Flower!" Molly chirped.

Iggy laughed under his breath, recalling the same name from one of Molly's favorite movies.

When Lily woke up from her nap, Mrs. Green got up from the rocking chair and put Lily in Iggy's lap once he sat down.

"Keep your arm behind her head, dear," Mrs. Green reminded Iggy.

Iggy remembered he had to hold Molly that way to support her neck when she was a newborn. Iggy looked down at the baby iguana and smiled. Lily smiled back.

"My turn!" Molly pulled on Iggy's tail.

"Patience doll. You're next in line." Mr. Green patted her on the head.

"Iggy's always first. And now I'm in the middle. I don't like this one bit." Molly ran out of the room and into her bedroom, coming back with her own baby doll instead.

Lily reached for Iggy's nose and cooed. She was wide-awake after sleeping in an egg for three months. Though he had just met her, Iggy realized that he already loved her.

3
TGIF ... or Not?

After three mornings of feeding his homework to Mr. Gruff, Iggy handed in his extra makeup work to his teacher when he arrived to school on Friday. By now Iggy was certain Mr. Gruff either liked the taste of his notebook paper or just had it in for him.

"Thank you young lizard." Looking over his spectacles, the goat examined the papers.

Iggy sat back down to start on his morning assignment, which was to read about some mockingbird who composed symphony number 40 ... and answer what seemed like a thousand questions afterward. Iggy was having a hard time concentrating on Mozart's story, not to mention he couldn't get over that he kept smelling skunk fumes. He spotted Samantha at Mr. Gruff's desk and figured he said something to upset her.

"Okay concentrate," he told himself.

"Shhhh," Isabella hissed.

"Sorry," he whispered.

Iggy looked over at Marc, who was busy memorizing the Pledge that he was *finally* able to give him after the mouse had been absent for three days.

"Pssst Marc. Where were you?" Iggy whispered.

"At the doctor," Marc said.

"For three days?"

"Well, I was in my *cama* too."

"*Cama*?" Iggy questioned.

Marc put his hands together like he was praying and put them under his cheek.

"Oh! Bed?" Iggy guessed.

"*Si*."

"Everything okay?" Iggy bit his lip. He knew Marc had some major health problems in the past, so hopefully it wasn't anything serious.

"I think so. They're always checking on me." Marc shrugged.

"So what was the matter then?"

"Nothing. Everything's good."

"Are you sure?" Iggy thought Marc looked really pale and seemed kind of tired. Marc just nodded.

Iggy had the slight suspicion Marc wasn't telling him everything and looked back down at his morning assignment. After re-reading the story, he decided to go ahead and try answering the questions. While twirling his pencil he couldn't help but think about the fact that Marc used a lot of energy on the field when they played soccer together the other day. Marc was breathing really hard after the game too, but Iggy figured it was because he was running so fast. Snap had told him that Marc was in something called *remission*, and he knew it had to do with cancer. Maybe Marc was allowed to wear his hat in class because his hair was falling out again. Iggy noticed he had on a new beanie hat, which Mr. Gruff still never made him take off.

Iggy sighed and returned to his questions and read

each one another time before answering. *Forget it*, he thought to himself and quickly scribbled down the best answer. Frustrated, he got out of his chair and turned in his morning assignment to Mr. Gruff, who was munching on Cooper's homework. Immediately Iggy saw the stack of graded quizzes on his teacher's desk. Iggy gulped. He was hoping Mr. Gruff wouldn't pass them back before the weekend, but sure enough right before lunch Mr. Gruff asked Cooper to hand back all of the quizzes.

When Cooper got to Iggy's desk he cringed. "Sorry, man." He put Iggy's quiz face down on his desk.

"What?" Iggy grabbed it and slowly turned the top front flap over. He closed one eye as if peeking would make matters better. When he saw the grade, his stomach dropped. Then his mouth dropped.

He quickly stuffed the paper in his desk, but then took it back out again just to make sure he wasn't seeing things. He had never failed a quiz before in his whole life.

He decided to flip through it, carefully making sure no one else saw all the red X's. This looked like the start to a horrible weekend. And as if matters couldn't get worse, Mr. Gruff announced that everyone had to get their quiz signed by a parent. The class groaned, grunted and croaked.

Iggy wanted to crawl inside his desk and hide. What was Mr. Gruff trying to do, get everyone in trouble? How was he going to tell his parents he failed?

Iggy walked home from school by himself that day since his mom had to rush Molly to her first Girl Scout meeting. Cooper, his next-door neighbor, had a guitar lesson and there was no point asking Liz. He wasn't in the mood to talk to anyone anyway.

Just before Iggy reached his house, he heard a loud roar of thunder. He looked up at the massive grey cloud over his head and a raindrop fell in his eye. "Seriously?"

Iggy blinked and rubbed his eye. Immediately the rain came down. He ran the rest of the way to his house and went inside as the lightning cracked. The house was dark and quiet, and the only thing heard in the background was the thunder.

Iggy walked upstairs to his room and plopped down on his bed. He turned on his Playbox 7 and played a baseball game ... until the power went out.

"Just great!" Iggy said out loud to the TV. He knew he should probably crack open a text book since he had nothing else to do, but instead Iggy stared out the window as his room echoed with silence.

At 5 o'clock the storm died down, and his power flashed back on. The phone rang with in a few seconds of his TV powering up. Iggy answered the phone, and his best friend, Snap Shell, was on the other line.

"Where ya been dude? I called a few times," Snap Shell said.

"You did? My power went out," Iggy said somberly. Normally he would have been more excited to talk to Snap.

"What's going on man? You sound like your bug died
or something."

"Nothing."

"Nothing? Really? Has the egg hatched yet?" Snap
asked.

"Yeah. It did the other day."

"Cool! What is it?"

"A girl," Iggy said.

"You don't sound too excited."

"I would have rather had a brother ya know ..."

"At least you have siblings man. I wish I had one."

Iggy changed the subject. "So how's sixth grade?"

"Sweet. All of the turtles you met out here are a year older than me, so I get to be in class with my friends. Plus, it's easy. I could have probably gone to seventh."

"Cool. You get bumped up a grade, and I'll probably get held back," Iggy said with a bit of sarcasm.

"What are you talking about brah? You still having problems with that donkey?"

"No ... goat."

"Oh, yeah. The goat," Snap laughed.

"I think he's got it in for me. I mean, I've had to re-do my homework everyday, and I even failed my first review quiz."

Snap's response was, "dude."

"Is that all you have to say?" Iggy sighed.

"No. I knew there was something going on," Snap said.

Iggy sat there in silence.

Snap went on. "Come on man! It's only the first week of school. Calm down."

"I'm going to fail!"

"No you're not. Why don't you just change the way you study?"

"How? Everything Mr. Gruff teaches is boring!" Iggy said.

"Let me guess, you've been daydreaming again?"

"Maybe."

"Well you're going to have to figure out a way to make it fun or you *are* going to fail dude."

"I don't know what to do."

"Think, man. What are you good at?" Snap asked.

"Like at school?"

"No. Like in general. What are you good at?"

"Um. Baseball?"

"Not just baseball. Think past baseball."

Iggy thought about it for a moment. Then he perked up. "Wait. Are you talking about when I hurt my arm and had to coach Liz instead of playing?" He yelled the last word into the phone.

"Dude! You're going to burst my eardrum. But yes, keep going."

"What does hurting myself have to do with Mr. Gruff and school though?"

"Coaching and teaching have a lot in common, Ig."

"I did teach Liz everything I know," Iggy said slowly.

"There ya go, brah. You're good at teaching," Snap confirmed.

"But how is that going to help me learn?"

"Seriously dude. Think about it. Some animals learn through teaching," Snap said.

"So, I need to teach this stuff to remember it?"

"Maybe."

"How? You want me to become the teacher or something?"

Snap cut him off. "Look, I can't fix everything, but believe me there's a better way to solve this problem. There's nothing wrong with you. You don't learn the same way as everyone else. It's not that big of a deal."

"What do you mean, I'm not like everyone else?" Iggy asked.

"You're killing me man. It's not a bad thing. You just need to be creative."

Iggy sat there still frustrated and still confused.

"Oh, hey. My pops is calling me downstairs. Hit me up and let me know how it all works out," Snap said.

"What? You have to go?"

"Sorry. See ya soon. Hang in there brah."

"See ya soon? Yeah right," Iggy said into the phone getting nothing back but a dial tone. Shaking his head, he hung up.

Just as Iggy was about to walk downstairs to see if dinner was ready, he heard his dad call out, "Iggy! Come downstairs. We need to talk to you."

4
It's All Mr. Gruff's Fault!

Iggy noticed his parents were particularly quiet when he sat down to dinner. After his mom dished out the meal on everyone's plate, his dad spoke up. "So we heard you got a quiz back today."

"Huh?" Iggy nearly dropped his fork.

"Dear is there something you need us to *sign*?" Mrs. Green asked.

"What?" Iggy's eyes were as big as two baseballs. He nodded *yes* without saying a word.

"Looks like we need to have a little talk after dinner," his dad said.

"Did Mr. Gruff call you?" Iggy shifted in his chair.

"Yes. During lunch," his mom answered. "But let's enjoy our meal together, and we can discuss it after dinner," his mom said and bowed her head, motioning to her husband to bless the food.

"Discuss what?" Molly chimed in.

"Nothing Molly. Put your head down," Iggy whispered.

After the prayer, Mr. Green turned to his wife to update her on a new client.

Molly was in her own little world as usual, humming to herself and separating each of her peas into groups.

Iggy couldn't hold it in anymore and blurted out. "It wasn't my fault!"

Mrs. Green stopped in mid-conversation with her husband. "Calm down dear. We'll discuss it after dinner."

Iggy sighed and picked at his food. Mr. Gruff should have minded his own business and let him tell his parents when he was ready. The weekend was ruined. His dad probably wouldn't take him to the batting cages now.

After dinner was over, Mr. Green told Molly to go upstairs to play. Iggy knew that meant it was time to get his quiz out of his backpack.

His parents motioned for him to come sit down with them on the couch. Iggy's mom took the quiz from Iggy and looked it over. As Iggy watched her flip through each page, he cringed at all the red. He watched his mom's eyes getting bigger and bigger. He couldn't even look at her when she got to the last page ... the page he practically left blank besides the picture he had drawn of a monkey hanging from a tree.

Mr. Green took the quiz, studied it and looked over at Iggy. "Nice picture son."

Trying to hold back a laugh, Iggy said, "Thanks."

"It's not funny. What's going on?"

"Nothing Dad. Mr. Gruff gave us a pop quiz on the first day of school. I couldn't remember *everything*!"

"But Mr. Gruff said you had the answers in your packet," his mother reminded him.

"Are you having problems paying attention?" his dad asked.

"No. It was only the first day of school!" Iggy wondered if he should just tell them he was bored.

"Your teacher said you've had to re-do your

homework every night this week. Maybe we should have a conference with him," his mom suggested.

"With Mr. Gruff? No!" Iggy yelled. "Can't you give me one more week?"

His dad got up from the couch. "We need to fix this problem before it gets worse son."

Iggy groaned, "I don't have a problem."

"Mr. Gruff says that you should try a few different things when you read and study."

"Mr. Gruff said that?" Iggy asked. "Like what?"

"He also said to cut back on your TV watching and game playing."

"Of course he did," Iggy said under his breath.

"Maybe you could have some of your friends come over to the house to study with you. You could make flashcards," Mrs. Green suggested.

"Flashcards? I'm not in first grade Mom."

"No, for a study group," Mrs. Green suggested.

"A study group? My friends aren't going to want to come over to study. They'll want to play my Playbox 7."

"Well, they won't be able to. Come on, you can even

serve refreshments. We've got plenty of Molly's Girl Scout cookies."

Iggy groaned, "This is turning into a play date."

Molly came running down the stairs. "What!? Those cookies aren't for his stinky friends! They're for *my* fundraiser!"

"Don't worry, I'll buy them. Go play." Mrs. Green shooed Molly along.

"But I want them!" Molly sat on the floor and pouted.

"What do you need so many cookies for?" Iggy asked.

"My tea parties!" Molly whined.

"You don't need all of those cookies young lady." Mrs. Green shook her head. "You need to learn to share."

"Yeah Molly. I thought Girl Scouts were supposed to be good role models," Iggy said.

Molly sat there for a second considering what her brother had said. "No, you're wrong. We just have to make the world a better place."

"Sharing *makes* the world a better place," Iggy said.

Mr. Green spoke up. "He does have a point."

"Maybe on the top of his head!" Molly shouted.

"Hey!" Iggy fixed his spike.

"You could help serve the cookies," their mom offered.

"Me? Serve? I don't think so."

"Well, I guess you won't meet your quota then," her dad said and sat down in his favorite chair.

"What? But I wanted to raise money for the butterflies." Molly paused for a moment and began tapping her press-on nails against her chin. "Well, I guess I can be his little waitress, but just this once."

Mr. Green smiled and changed the subject back to Iggy's quiz. "I think you should try to find the answers to the questions you missed and turn it back in to Mr. Gruff. We can go over it together when you're finished."

"Fine," Iggy sighed and walked up to his room. He was getting all too use to re-doing his work. He started to wonder if a study group would help him.

♦ ♦ ♦

To Iggy's surprise the next morning, his dad woke him up to go to the batting cages. "We're still going?" Iggy said as he sat up in his bed and rubbed his eyes.

"Of course, Champ. Why wouldn't we?"

"Well, I figured since, well ... you know ..."

"I think you should relieve some of that school stress on a baseball," Mr. Green said.

Iggy couldn't agree more and got up to get ready.

After breakfast, Iggy and his dad grabbed all of their gear and drove to the batting cages. The last time he had been to the cages was with Snap, before his arm injury. His head flooded with memories.

"What's wrong son? You don't look too excited. Still upset about your quiz?" Mr. Green asked when they got out of the car.

Iggy looked up at his dad. "This place reminds me of Snap."

"I know you miss your best friend son. Have you made any new friends at school?"

"Yeah, there's a new kid named Sid. He's nice, but I hang out with Marc most of the time."

"How's Marc doing?" Mr. Green asked as he opened up the back of the car to get the baseball gear out.

"He was absent from school for most of the week

because he said he was at the doctor. I asked him if he was okay, and he said yes, but he didn't look good."

"Oh, really?" Mr. Green stopped what he was doing and put the gear on the ground after shutting the trunk.

"Do you know what's wrong with him Dad?"

"I know a little bit. His dad and I have been friends for a while. Marc was diagnosed with Leukemia when he was still living in Madrid, Spain. Even though Marc's cancer went into remission, he still needs to be in Houston to get checked on in case it comes back."

"I don't really understand remission," Iggy said.

Mr. Green looked down at Iggy and said, "Well, it means that the cancer cells are no longer detected."

"No longer detected? So if the cancer cells are gone, why do they call it remission? Why don't they just say he's cured?" Iggy asked.

Mr. Green put his hand on Iggy's shoulder and sighed, "He's not exactly cured. There's something called a relapse, where the cancer can come back even with the treatment. Some animals may need a bone marrow transplant to get better."

"So it can come back then?" Iggy was trying to understand.

"Yes, but the goal is to actually keep the body in remission. So it's important that if Marc still needs treatment, he gets it to keep the cancer from coming back."

"But what if it doesn't work?" Iggy asked.

His father stepped back and took in a deep breath. He slowly let it out. "Let's first think positively son. We don't know what's going on with Marc yet. That's why we have really talented doctors looking out for him."

"Is there anything we can do for him?" Iggy asked.

"Of course," his dad said. "We can pray for him."

Iggy stood there for a moment and looked up at the blue sky. "Then that's what I'm going to do."

"I'm sure Marc will appreciate that." Mr. Green smiled and pulled down the rim of Iggy's baseball cap below his eyes. "Race you to the batting cage."

"Hey! No fair!" Iggy grabbed his gear bag and ran after his father. He felt better about Marc after talking to his dad.

Once the iguanas got inside and checked in, Mr. Green motioned for Iggy to head to the slow pitch cage to get his timing down. The first few hits felt a bit stiff since it had been a while since the last time he swung a bat.

Mr. Green reminded Iggy to follow through and not baby his arm. After a few rounds, Iggy started to feel comfortable again.

"Want to try the fast pitch, son?" his dad questioned.

"Do you think I'm ready?"

"You're the only one who can answer that. How's your pain?"

"My arm's tighter than normal, but no pain," Iggy said.

"Let's give it a go then! One round."

Both iguanas walked over to the fast pitch and put in a few coins. Iggy wiggled his bat above his head and planted his foot. He watched the first two go by to see what the machine was going to do. He swung at the rest, hitting hard and strong.

"Nice job, son. That's the way to do it! We should stop by the field on the way home to throw some balls."

Iggy felt good about his batting, but the big test would be his pitching, which was the cause of his injury. He hoped his pitcher's elbow wouldn't flare up, but that didn't stop him from saying, "Let's go!"

Once they got to Memorial Field, Iggy looked at the empty bleachers and imagined the crowd. Being back on the field felt so good. The smell, the hot Texas sun on his scales and the dirt under his feet made him forget all about his issues at school. So far the day had been perfect. Iggy stared off into the distance at a few lizards walking up to the field.

"Wait a minute," Iggy said. "Liz?"

"Looks like Liz and Coach Brown had the same idea for their Saturday," Mr. Green said and walked toward the lizards.

"Hey Iggy. Hi Coach Green!" Liz said and gave Iggy's dad a hug.

Iggy looked down when Liz looked his way.

"Why don't you two go throw a few while Coach Green and I have a chat," Coach Brown suggested and waved the kids on.

"You wanna?" Liz asked.

"Sure," Iggy shrugged, still not making eye contact with her. Iggy tossed the ball back and forth in his glove as he walked to center field with Liz by his side. He kept quiet, not knowing what to talk about with the lizard anymore.

"So, how's your arm doing?" Liz broke the silence.

"Okay, I guess."

"Oh, yeah?"

"Yeah."

"So ..." Liz crossed her arms.

The two of them stood there in silence.

"So what?" Iggy questioned, thinking this was a weird conversation.

"Are we going to throw balls or not?" she asked.

"Oh, I didn't know you still liked baseball," Iggy smirked and turned his head as if he saw something interesting across the field.

"What's *that* supposed to mean?" Liz questioned.

Iggy knew he was asking for it now. "Nothing."

"Spit it out. What are you trying to say?"

"You ... you're all girly now. You know," Iggy said, noticing the confused look on her face he went on, "you and Isabella and your makeup and stuff."

"Seriously? Give me that ball!" She grabbed the ball out of Iggy's glove and walked across the field. Iggy followed.

The lizards threw the ball back and forth for a while, until Iggy spoke up. "So do you think Isabella will try out for softball with you next year?" Iggy laughed, clearly knowing the answer to that question.

"Don't be silly. Izzy wouldn't be caught a hundred feet near a dirty, dusty field with sweaty animals," Liz said and threw the ball to Iggy.

"Izzy?" Iggy caught it and threw her a fastball.

Liz reacted quickly and snagged the ball. "Yeah. Isabella," she yelled.

"You call her *Izzy* now? It's only been a week, and you and *Izzy* are like BFFs!" Iggy said.

"Whatever! I can tell you guys don't like her that much, well except Cooper," Liz said rolling her eyes.

"It's not that I don't like her," Iggy said. "She's just not my type."

Liz laughed. "Your type? So what is your type then?"

"That's not what I meant."

"What *did* you mean?" she asked and threw the ball back.

"I don't know."

Liz smirked. "I know she can be kinda stuck up ..."

Iggy cut her off. "Ya think?"

"And I know she brags a lot. But just try to give her a chance. Please?" Liz asked.

Iggy stood there and thought about it. "Maybe, but only on one condition."

"What?" Liz grinned.

"You have to walk home with me from school every once in a while."

Liz started to giggle. "Okay, okay. It's a deal. You must have really missed me, huh?"

"No." He blushed and changed the subject. "Ready to head in?"

"Already?" Liz asked. "Sure, if you're ready."

"Yeah, I've got homework to do."

"We didn't have homework, except to get our quiz signed."

Iggy didn't want to admit that he failed the quiz or that his parents were making him do extra work. "I just meant I should take it easy ... you know with my arm and all."

"Whatever you say coach." Liz winked at him and skipped away to meet her dad.

5
Call 911

After spending the rest of the weekend locked in his room reading and making trivia note cards, Iggy was looking forward to getting out of the house and being around animal life again at school.

On Monday morning, his mom handed him a stack of flyers before he left for school.

"What are these?" Iggy asked.

"Flyers for your study group," she said and winked.

"Mom! I don't need to give my friends flyers. I'll just tell them about it."

"Just use them honey. They have all the information your friend's parents will need to know."

Iggy read the flyer. "You are *cordially* invited? Seriously?" Iggy sighed. He really didn't want to pass out *mom-made* flyers. It seemed a little embarrassing.

Mrs. Green had a big smile on her face. Iggy could tell she was proud of her crafty invitations, so he put the flyers in his backpack and left for school with his sister.

Once Iggy got to class that morning, he pulled his corrected quiz and his note cards out of his backpack and walked straight up to Mr. Gruff's desk.

"May I help you Iggy?" Mr. Gruff was finishing his daily paper, so basically eating breakfast.

"I fixed all of the answers." Iggy handed the quiz with his mom's signature to his teacher.

Mr. Gruff examined the paper and flipped through each section, making sounds like, "Hmmmm" and "Ahuh." Iggy stood there not knowing whether to look at Mr. Gruff or around the room, so he did a combination of both.

"Very well Iggy, I will change your grade from an F to a D+," Mr. Gruff said and put the papers in his drawer.

"D plus?" Iggy said under his breath.

"Is there a problem?"

Iggy fumbled with the note cards in his hand. He appreciated the grade change, but it was still a bad grade, and he was hoping Mr. Gruff would have raised it more if he was going to raise it at all. "No," he said.

"Is there anything more you would like to show me?" Mr. Gruff said and looked down at Iggy's hand.

"Oh. I made these over the weekend." Iggy handed the note cards to his teacher.

"A game, huh?" Mr. Gruff flipped through the cards.

"Trivia," Iggy gulped.

"I see you're thinking outside the box. Is there anything else?"

Iggy couldn't tell if Mr. Gruff's straight face was impressed or disappointed. He was so hard to read.

"No. That's all."

"Very well. Please start on your morning work. We have much to do. My favorite unit starts today, U. S. Government," Mr. Gruff said, handing Iggy back his cards.

Iggy forced a smile and walked back to his seat.

"What'sssss that?" Sid asked and uncoiled a section

of his body while sitting in mid-air with his head only an inch away from Iggy's face.

"Oh, hey Sid," Iggy said, startled. He still wasn't used to Sid's whole floating back and forth thing.

Sid shook his rattle in response.

"Just some note cards."

"Cardssssss?"

"Yeah, I made them for social studies. See, here's one about the Bill of Rights."

"Oh. Sssssssmart idea."

"Would you want to be in my study group then?" Iggy asked since Sid seemed interested.

"A sssssstudy group?" Sid questioned.

Iggy hesitated to respond and put the note cards back in his backpack. "I know it's a dumb idea."

"I would love to be in your sssssstudy group!"

"Really?" Iggy said surprised. "Cool!" He considered giving Sid a flyer right then, but decided to wait until lunchtime.

Sid's neck and head floated back to his seat, and Iggy started on his morning work.

Mr. Gruff wasn't joking when he said his favorite unit was U.S. Government. The goat went on and on about The Constitution, like he was one of the animals who signed the thing. Mr. Gruff took everything so seriously, especially history and even more so, classroom rules. He wouldn't let the class leave the room for lunch until everyone was in a perfectly straight line. Iggy didn't understand why straight lines really mattered that much, but Mr. Gruff always went on and on about how following directions precisely was a necessary trait of successful animals in the real world. It never failed, Cooper usually caused the class to be five minutes late to lunch everyday due to his constant fidgeting and his camouflaging while in line.

Once the animals were seated at the lunch table, Iggy passed out a flyer to each of his friends.

"What in the world is this?" Kit Kat meowed. "A study group? I don't need to study in a group. I work alone."

"Who made these?" Cooper read Iggy's flyer out loud. "You are cordially invited to a weekly study group at the Greens. Snacks and refreshments served."

"Snacks? What kind of snacks?" Kit Kat looked back down at his own copy.

"Well, my sister's selling Girl Scout cookies and has a lemonade stand in her bedroom," Iggy explained.

"Wait. Do we have to pay to be in the group to eat? Is this like some kind of fundraising Girl Scout cookie trick to get us to buy cookies?" Buddy croaked.

"No! My mom already has the cookies," Iggy sighed.

"I think it sounds like a great idea," Liz said.

"You do??" Isabella looked at Liz and snarled.

"What if we all start today after school?" Liz suggested.

"Okay, but only if your sister has those caramel chocolate cookies. Those are my favorites," Kit Kat said while stuffing an Oreo in his mouth.

"Yeah, she has those," Iggy said.

Isabella pursed her lips and spoke up. "We can use my extra room above the gym in my house. It's basically like my own apartment. My nanny can make the cookies from scratch."

"Yeah, we should go to Isabella's!" Cooper said gazing like a love struck lizard.

"No! Iggy has Playbox 7!" Buddy spoke up.

Iggy rolled his eyes. He knew his friends would only want to play video games once they came over.

"Playbox 7? I have a Playbox 10!" Isabella said.

Buddy turned quickly to the iguana. "What? I've never even heard of a Playbox 10. Besides, there aren't any games out for that one."

"I have the games!" Isabella retorted.

"I think you're lying," Buddy said as he ate his flies.

Liz decided to speak up. "It's Iggy's group, let's just go over to *his* house."

"Like I said, only if you have the caramel ones. If not, I'm out," Kit Kat stated as his final offer.

"I promise you *all* will get all the cookies you can eat. So is everyone in or not?" Iggy looked around the table at his friends. Everyone agreed to ask their parents and head over after school.

Once Iggy got home that afternoon, his mom offered to help Molly set up her lemonade stand in the game room, while he got his study material ready. As Iggy put the last chair around the table, the doorbell rang. He ran downstairs and opened the door to Kit Kat. The cat came in and looked around the room with the eyes of a starving dog searching for a hidden bone.

"Don't worry. They're upstairs," Iggy laughed while shaking his head.

Before Kit Kat and Iggy headed up, Cooper and Buddy showed up. Iggy opened up the door again. "Hey guys. Molly's got everything upstairs in the game room."

Mrs. Green took the guys upstairs while Iggy waited for the girls, Sid and Marc.

Once everyone arrived, Molly handed each of her guests a pink polka dotted napkin. "Welcome to *Café Molly!*" Molly said and curtsied. When Molly handed Liz her napkin, she instantly commented on the lizard's new look. "Nice gloss," Molly said. She grabbed for Isabella's rhinestone purse, and Isabella pulled back.

"Careful. Those are designer rhinestones," Isabella said arrogantly.

"Pul-lease. Everyone knows rhinestones are fake." Molly started to hand Isabella a napkin, but dropped it before Isabella could take it. She casually walked behind her lemonade stand and started serving the refreshments. Once everyone got their serving, and Kit Kat got seconds, they took their seats around a huge coffee table, and Mrs. Green went back downstairs to feed Lily.

Iggy thumbed through his note cards as his friends chatted and messed around on their cell phones. He wasn't really sure where to begin, and that's when he realized he had no idea what he was doing. Everyone expected him to lead the group. He tried to remember what Snap said. *Coaching and teaching were like baseball, and Iggy was good at baseball.*

"No, that's not right!" Iggy said.

"Who are you talking to?" Cooper asked.

"Oh, no one, I'm just trying to get everything ready in my head." He fumbled through his note cards again and could feel his cheeks getting hot. He knew he was going to have to eventually quiet everyone down to begin, but he didn't really know what he wanted to say.

"Hey, man. You're turning red. I thought I was the only lizard here who could do that." Cooper was the first to notice.

"Shhhh." Liz nudged Cooper in his side. "So what are we going to start with, Iggy?" she asked.

Kit Kat took the liberty to answer. "Well, we have a test on Friday on the branches of government, in case you all forgot." Kit Kat smirked and took a gulp from his lemonade, then crossed his legs.

Iggy spoke up. "Right! I was thinking we should play a review game like we used to do in fourth grade!"

"Yeah! Whatever happened to playing review games? Mr. Gruff doesn't do anything fun!" Buddy blurted out.

"No kidding! He's the worst teacher I've ever had," Kit Kat said.

"And the meanest," Buddy added.

"You're both mad because you didn't turn in your homework, and he gave you a zero!" Isabella yelled and did her typical fish-face look at the boys.

"How would you know what we made?" Buddy asked.

Isabella smirked, grabbed a brush out of her purse and started brushing her hair spikes at the table. "I stayed after to help Mr. Gruff grade papers."

"What? You really *are* a suck up!" Kit Kat meowed.

"I can't help it if Mr. Gruff likes me more than you! Not to mention ... I'm smarter."

"Well, in that case Miss Know-it-all, why don't you teach the branches of government to everyone?" Kit Kat boldly took a bite out of another cookie.

"How many of those cookies are you going to eat anyway?" Isabella snapped at the cat.

"How many times are you going to remind us how awesome you are?" Kit Kat mocked her.

"Alright guys. We don't have time to argue." Iggy cut them both off. Their arguing kind of took the focus off his anxiety.

"Whatever! You all are so boring. I'm leaving!" Isabella turned to Liz. "Are you coming or what?"

Everyone turned to Liz. Liz glanced at Iggy and gave him a reassuring look. "I'm staying."

"FINE. I don't need to be in this little study group anyway." Isabella stormed out of the room, tripping on one of Molly's high heels as she darted down the stairs. "Urrrrr!" She slammed the door as she exited dramatically.

"Wow!" Cooper curled his tail in and out. "Did that *seriously* just happen? What crawled up her tail?"

Liz shrugged. "She gets like that sometimes."

"Okay. Well now that that's over we should probably get started," Iggy said to the group. However, that plan instantly failed once Molly entered the scene with a caged dragonfly. Molly leaped onto the table and sprinkled glitter on everyone's head.

"What is this stuff?" Kit Kat coughed.

"Fairy dust! Duh! I'm here to grant one of you a wish," Molly said.

"How about another cookie? That's my wish." Kit Kat nudged Cooper.

"Molly! Can't you see we're working?" Iggy stood up and grabbed for his sister's tutu.

"Please. You all haven't done a thing. I've been watching this whole time." Molly gracefully hopped to the floor and opened up the door to Tink's cage. Cooper and Buddy eyed the dragonfly and started to wet their lips.

"Molly! What are you doing? That fly can't be loose in the house," Iggy yelled.

"Fly?" Molly paused and looked directly at her brother. "Tink demands an apology. She's not a fly. Flies eat their own ..."

Iggy cut her off. "Fine a fairy. But I promise this is *not* a good idea," Iggy said as he recognized the looks in the frog and chameleon's eyes. "Don't even think about it," he said and glared at Buddy and Cooper.

Molly stuck her hand inside the cage and Tink hopped onto her finger. "See! She's trained."

Everyone got up from their chairs to take a look at Tink and watch her do her tricks. Molly told her to leap, and the dragonfly jumped off her finger and landed on her nose. Then Molly commanded her to fly, and Tink flew around the room in a circle and landed back on Molly's shoulder.

"I told you she's trained." Molly looked at Iggy.

"That may have been the coolest thing I've ever seen," Cooper said and walked up closer to the dragonfly.

Liz held out her finger and Tink hopped on.

"She likes girls more than boys." Molly winked at Liz.

"Can I try?" Cooper asked.

"No. We're running out of time. Molly, please take your fairy back to its kingdom," Iggy said and looked over at the chameleon who was literally drooling. "Now Molly!"

"Cooper wants a turn," Molly said and smirked.

"That's not a good ..."

Before Iggy had a chance, the chameleon shot out his tongue. Tink flew straight toward Molly, and Cooper's

tongue hit the little iguana right between the eyes.

Molly's eyes crossed and she screamed while wiping off her face. "GROSS!" Tink went flying around the room, and the chameleon ran after her.

"Leave her alone you barbarian!" Molly yelled and grabbed Cooper by the tail with all of her strength, attempting to hold him back.

Cooper tried to catch the dragonfly once more, but missed again, and his tongue smacked against the wall. Tink made a quick escape and flew into Molly's room. Molly let go of Cooper's tail, which sent him crashing into the wall, and Molly went running after her dragonfly, screaming, "Call 911! Call 911!"

6
Camouflaged

Iggy looked directly at the chameleon whose tongue was still stuck to the side of the wall. "Are you crazy?"

"What?" Cooper jerked his head back, taking off a piece of wall paint with his sticky tongue.

Mrs. Green came running upstairs. "What in the world is going on?"

Molly ran out of her room, crying, "Dragonfly slayer!"

"Calm down, Molly. What's the matter?" Mrs. Green asked.

Molly pointed directly at Cooper. "Him! Cooper tried to eat Tink!"

Mrs. Green turned to Cooper.

"Sorry Mrs. Green. I couldn't resist." Cooper shrugged casually. "I'll go."

"That's probably a good idea Cooper," Mrs. Green said, shaking her head.

Buddy followed after him.

"Why are you leaving?" Iggy asked.

"He's my ride."

"Your ride? He lives next door."

"I know, but I'm having dinner at his house. Sauteed flies," Buddy said and hopped away.

Iggy sighed and sauntered back to the head of the table. Once the group got back in their seats, Iggy was about to ask everyone who made up the executive branch, but Kit Kat's cell phone rang. They all waited as he had what seemed like a ten minute conversation with his mother.

"Okay, okay Mom. I told you we're studying. Wait, what? Lasagna? Okay, I'll be outside in a minute," Kit Kat said and ended his phone call.

"How did you get your cell phone back?" Iggy asked when the cat hung up.

"I have my ways. Sorry guys! Gotta go," he said and brushed the crumbs off his chair.

Iggy looked around at the sad remains of his study group. "Okay, so as we were saying," Iggy kept on. "The President is a part of the executive branch, and so is the ..." He got cut off again, but this time by Liz's cell phone. "When did *you* get a cell phone?" Iggy asked.

Liz answered her phone. "Hey Izzy. What's up?"

Iggy huffed and looked at Marc. "Why is Isabella calling when she knows Liz is studying with us?"

Marc shrugged and got up from his chair but with hesitation.

"Wait, where are you going?" Iggy asked.

"I'm going to go visit my *amigo* at the hospital. I meant to tell you I needed to leave early," Marc said.

"Fine, go ahead." Iggy couldn't be mad at Marc.

Liz got up from her chair. "Sorry Iggy, but Isabella's dad is getting us advanced movie screening passes to *Wizard Lizards* tonight."

"What? No way? I didn't know they were making that into a movie!" Iggy gasped.

"Yeah, I wish you could go with us," Liz said and crinkled her nose. "But she only has two tickets. Good study group though." Liz got up and hurried downstairs.

Sid nervously looked at Iggy and shook his rattle. Iggy looked at Sid and then at all the empty chairs. "Fine, you can go too."

Sid bit his lip and slithered downstairs, leaving Iggy at the coffee table with his note cards. So much for his mom's great idea to start a study group. He was back to studying on his own, which never worked.

◆　◆　◆

Molly wouldn't even come down to breakfast the next morning. She refused to leave Tink by herself and even insisted that she stay home from school to counsel Tink and help her through her anxiety.

While Iggy was finishing his breakfast, his mom sat down in the seat across from him. "Have you apologized to your sister yet?"

"Apologize? Mom, it wasn't my idea. I told you the study group wouldn't work!"

"Calm down dear. It would have worked if your friend showed some manners. I don't know what it is about that Cooper kid."

"Mom. He eats flies. Tink's basically a dumb fly!"

Mr. Green walked into the kitchen. "Son. You don't need to talk to your mom like that. I know boys can be boys, but it was still wrong. Be the bigger animal and try to understand your sister's point of view. She loves that bug."

Iggy just sat there. If his mom didn't make him start the study group, this would have never happened.

"At least try to cheer your sister up. She's very upset," his mom said.

"Fine," Iggy groaned. That was not going to be easy, so he picked a little white flower from the front lawn, went upstairs and knocked on Molly's door.

Molly peeked out her door with only one eyeball and asked, "Who's there?"

"Molly, you know who it is!"

"How dare you come. Who sent you?" she questioned.

"I have something for your dragonfly's cage."

"Cage? Never insult Tink like that. No thanks to you

she's traumatized for the rest of her life!" Molly shut the door in Iggy's face.

He knocked again. "Come on Molly. I promise she'll like it. It's tiny ... just like Tink."

Molly yanked open the door, pulled Iggy quickly inside and dramatically looked down the hall to make sure no one else was around. He handed her the tiny flower.

"Seriously. This?" Molly flicked the flower with her finger. That's a weed! Tink is disgusted by weeds." She pointed her nose in the air.

"Whatever Molly. I should have just given you back Ramon the Roach, who you gave me for my birthday. He would have made a great date for your dumb fairy fly."

"Get out!" Molly pointed toward the door.

Iggy bit his lip. This was not going well. "Okay, okay. I'm sorry Cooper's such a ... such a ..."

Molly cut him off. "Pig!"

"A what? Don't use words like that. Pigs don't eat any more than we do. Just come down for breakfast. You're making mom go crazy. It's enough that she has to take care of a baby, but now you're acting like one too."

"No I'm not! All of this is the egg's fault anyway. I don't ever want to see that thing again."

"What? How is this Lily's fault? And you don't have to call our sister an egg anymore. She did hatch remember?"

"You're right, this is *your* fault!"

"No Molly, it's your fault for bringing Tink out and interrupting the study group."

"Whatever! You're making me late for school." Molly darted past Iggy and ran downstairs.

"So that's it?" Iggy rolled his eyes and left the room.

♦　♦　♦

That day at school was just the same as the others. Mr. Gruff scolded the usual troublemakers and demanded that everyone keep their desks in perfectly straight rows. By now Iggy was certain Mr. Gruff was obsessed with straight lines. Kit Kat and Digger Dog almost got into a cat and dog fight in the lunch line over the last piece of corn loaf, until the lunch lady wacked them both over the head with a stinky wet rag. Isabella was bragging about something or other of absolutely no importance at recess.

The next day and the day after were pretty much the same as the one before. His classes continued to get harder and more boring if that was even possible. Iggy left school feeling more discouraged than when he got there. The only thing that was different was his walks home from school. Cooper started tagging along, which enraged Molly.

"Come on Molly! You have to forgive me some day," Cooper said and tried to pull off a disappearing act to impress her.

"You can't even camouflage correctly. Some kind of chameleon you are!" Molly put her nose up in the air and picked up her pace, leaving the boys following behind her.

"Your sister is a tough one."

"I heard that!" Molly yelled without looking back.

"You think I don't know that?" Iggy said.

"I'm going to tell mom you're hanging out with a troublemaker Iggy! You know she doesn't like him!"

"What? Your mom doesn't like me?"

"No. Molly's always a brat." Iggy tried to reassure him. He didn't think Cooper was *that* bad. He had a zany sense of humor, and Iggy was starting to see that he and Cooper had a lot in common. They both loved sports, they'd rather be outdoors than stuck in a classroom, and they were both having trouble paying attention in class. Cooper even told Iggy that he caught that concentration problem once, so he had a good excuse for misbehaving.

"Are you sure you're not just bored?" Iggy asked.

"Of course I'm bored. I'm always bored."

"Me too, but there's gotta be a way to get through it though ... right?"

"No. I've just got a problem. It's cool though. I'm going to be a professional baseball player," Cooper said.

"But what if you get hurt?"

"What does it matter?"

"I don't know, I mean what if you can't get a job? Then what?"

"Iggy, I'm only twelve. I'll figure something out when I get older. Besides, it's not like I need to know anything about democracy and Congress right now."

"What? You're twelve?" Iggy gasped.

"Yeah. So what?"

"Shouldn't you be in the sixth grade then?" Iggy questioned.

"I'm repeating fifth grade again. I learned the same stuff at my old school last year."

"Are you serious?" Iggy blurted out.

"What does it matter?"

Iggy began to see that Cooper didn't care about much of anything. "So when did you just stop trying?" he asked.

Cooper stopped in front of Iggy's house and stood there. "What are you trying to say?" Cooper asked and took on the shade of the tree trunk behind him.

"Um. Nothing." Iggy wasn't sure if he should repeat the question because Cooper was acting strange.

"You think I'm dumb, huh?" Cooper yelled.

"What? No! Of course I don't! I asked you when you stopped trying?"

"Oh." Cooper closed his eyes and completely blended into the tree. That was the first time Iggy saw the chameleon's disappearing act actually work. It was pretty amazing.

After a few moments of complete silence, Iggy said, basically to the tree, "You're not dumb Cooper."

"Why don't you tell my dad that?" Cooper turned back into his normal multi color shade.

"Wait, your dad said that to you?" Iggy asked.

"Yeah. But who cares. I know I am," the chameleon said and quickly changed the subject. "Hey want to play Playbox 7 at your house?" Cooper asked.

"Cooper! We've got a test tomorrow!"

"I don't care." The chameleon turned around and walked home.

So maybe Iggy didn't agree with everything Cooper said, but listening to Cooper and his excuses started to make Iggy think about his own issues differently. He couldn't believe Cooper's own dad would call him dumb. Iggy couldn't imagine either of his parents *ever* calling him such an awful thing.

Iggy had to find a new way of studying, and he needed to figure it out fast. He wanted to do something to make learning fun so he wouldn't feel so discouraged. Plus, he didn't want to repeat fifth grade again. Unfortunately he only had one night before his first test, so he pulled out his note cards and went over the same boring material the way he had every night before.

1
Something Smells Funny

The urge to throw up kept hitting Iggy on the walk to school Friday morning. He ran over to a neighbor's bush twice, but it was a false alarm.

"What's wrong with you?" Molly asked.

"You'll understand when you get older," Iggy said. He couldn't believe his nerves were literally making him sick. Iggy decided to start repeating everything he memorized for the test. He needed to go through it one more time, and maybe it would help him keep his mind off his upset stomach.

"I don't want to hear about check outs and balance beams," Molly groaned.

"It's checks and balances Molly. They balance out the branches of government."

"Like I care," Molly said and started humming an obnoxious tune.

By the time Iggy got to class, he was sweating, his head was pounding and he was considering visiting the bathroom, *again*. He walked past Mr. Gruff who was chewing on a Styrofoam coffee cup and scribbling instructions in some form of chicken scratch on the board.

Get in your seats
Take out a No. 2 pencil
No Cheating!!!!!!

Mr. Gruff handed a stack of test packets with answer sheets to each of the students in the front row to pass back. When Iggy looked down at the top packet, there were only three questions per page due to the fact every question was a paragraph long. This was not going to be good. Iggy gulped and handed the rest of the tests to Isabella.

He took a deep breath, wrote his name on the front page and read the first question about the Constitution. He felt a bead of sweat start to form on his forehead and his stomach tighten. It didn't make sense. Was it talking about ratifying it? And why couldn't these questions have been multiple choice?

He remembered reading a note card about the Constitution, but now he wished he would have re-read the whole section in his book about it again. What he should have done was found a way to teach someone or talked about it with his dad. Why didn't he think of these things before? Why was he thinking about more ways to study while taking the test?

Iggy looked at the clock and realized eight minutes had passed, and he hadn't even answered the first question. He had to get himself together. *Just concentrate*, he told himself, while taking in a deep breath and writing down what he remembered for each question. Even if he had to guess, maybe he would get some credit. Wait, he was talking about Mr. Gruff here.

When Mr. Gruff gave a ten-minute warning, Iggy had

five more questions to go. He guessed on the last two, but he was pretty sure he got the other three correct. Iggy went back over his work looking for mistakes. No telling how many points Mr. Gruff would take off for spelling, even though it wasn't a spelling test. That's just the kind of goat he was.

Iggy walked up to Mr. Gruff's desk to turn in his test.

"Did you finish this time Iggy?"

Iggy gulped. "Yes, sir."

Mr. Gruff looked over his spectacles and smiled. Iggy did a double take, but the moment passed, and Mr. Gruff looked back down at his paperwork.

After all the tests were turned in, the class lined up for lunch, and Mr. Gruff made an announcement: "All students who make a C or below on the test will be pulled out of lunch next week for tutoring. Enjoy your lunch!"

Iggy watched Cooper roll his eyes and say, "What's next? He's going to visit us at home to make sure we're doing our homework?"

"Right!" Kit Kat meowed.

Once the kids got to the lunchroom, the group talked about the test for a few minutes until Buddy changed the subject. "So what's everyone doing this weekend? Anyone want to hang out?" he croaked.

Isabella was the first to answer. "I'm going to Austin tomorrow."

"Let me guess. Your dad has a lake house?" Kit Kat rolled his eyes.

"Why yes, on Lake Travis." She smirked and looked at Liz. "Want to come?"

Liz avoided eye contact with the rest of the group while responding. "I'll ask my parents," she whispered.

"I'm not doing anything. I can hang," Cooper said as he stole a fly from Buddy's lunch.

"Me either. Besides a hair cut," Kit Kat said and licked his paw to comb back his hair.

"Maybe we can go to that new game store by my house," Buddy said. "The new Pro Ball Showdown is out!"

"You don't even have a PlayBox 7 yet," Kit Kat laughed.

"Iggy does though!" Buddy said. "Hey, will your dad let you buy Pro Ball Showdown?"

Iggy finally spoke up. "Maybe. But I can't go. I'm going to Galveston Beach with my cousin."

"Dragon D?" Liz asked.

"Yeah."

"Who's Dragon D?" Cooper looked up from his fruit tray.

"A water dragon," Iggy said.

"Can he drive?" Cooper asked.

"Yeah," Iggy said.

"Cool! I want to go!" Cooper curled out his tail and quickly curled it back in.

"Okay. I'll ask my cousin, but I'm sure he'll say yes," Iggy said.

"Me too! I've never been to Galveston, *and* I've never met a dragon." Buddy hopped up from his chair. "Then he can take us to the store on the way back!"

"How have you never been to Galveston?" Cooper asked.

"He used to live in New York," Kit Kat blurted out with

his mouth full of food and kept on, "So is it going to be really hot in Galveston?"

"You can jump in the water," Iggy said.

"Jump in the water? I sir ... am a cat."

Iggy looked at Marc. "You wanna go?"

"I probably can't." Marc shrugged and kept eating his pudding.

"What about you Sid?" Iggy asked.

"Sssssssorry. I wish I could go, but the ssssssnakes on my dad'sssss ssssssside of the family are coming in for a reunion.

Iggy pictured in his head what a house full of snakes would look like and shivered.

The honey badger came up behind Iggy, blew her whistle and yelled, "Line up!"

The animals jumped and scurried to throw away their trash before she made them clean off the entire lunch table with a smelly rag.

When Iggy got back to Mr. Gruff's class that afternoon, the goat was already walking around the room handing back tests. Iggy thought for sure his teacher wouldn't have had time to grade all those tests, but leave it to Mr. Gruff to get the job done.

The same sick feeling he had earlier occurred in his stomach as Mr. Gruff approached his desk. "Good try Iggy. You'll do better next time." Mr. Gruff laid the test face down.

"Good try? " Iggy flipped over his test immediately.

C -

It looked like he earned himself a ticket into Mr. Gruff's lunch tutoring session. The bell rang and Iggy slowly dragged himself to his locker.

Liz came up to Iggy and nudged him. "How'd you do on the test?" she asked and crinkled her brow.

"Okay, I guess," Iggy shrugged and shut his locker.

"Want to walk home together?"

"Really?" Iggy asked. "Is your *BFF* walking with us?"

"Nah. She's got something to do. It's just you and me kid."

"Okay. I just need to make sure Molly's going home

with Little Bit." Iggy also knew Cooper had his guitar lesson on Fridays, so it would actually be nice to talk to Liz.

Once Iggy checked on his sister, and she was good to go, the lizards headed home. The first words out of Liz's mouth were, "I'd rather go with you guys to Galveston instead of Izzy's lake house."

"Why don't you then?" Iggy questioned.

"I don't want to deal with Izzy getting mad at me again," the lizard sighed.

"Again? When did she get mad at you?"

"That day at your house when I didn't leave with her."

"But she asked you to go see *Wizard Lizards*."

"I know. It was awesome too."

"Girls are *so* confusing," Iggy said.

"Yeah, it's complicated."

"Obviously," Iggy said.

"So is everything okay?" Liz asked out of nowhere.

"What? With me?" Iggy was caught off guard.

"Um. Yeah ... who else?"

"Yeah. I'm cool. Why would you ask that?"

"I know you. Something's up." Liz had a worried look on her face.

"It's not a big deal. I just don't really like school this year."

"Is it Mr. Gruff?" Liz asked.

"Yeah, I guess. Don't you think he's hard with all his make-up work and quizzes?"

"Yeah, but it doesn't bother me." Liz shrugged.

"Well, it sure bothers me. I thought I failed again!"

"Again?" she asked.

"I'm just kidding." Iggy wanted to shut his mouth and change the subject.

Liz stood there with another weird look on her face.

"What? I mean I'll be fine," he said and looked down.

"If you need help studying, let me know." Liz nudged him.

"Really? You want to study with me?"

"Sure!" She batted her eyelashes.

Iggy froze. He suddenly felt very uncomfortable. Was Liz making googly eyes at him? He started counting down the houses and realized his dad's car was in front of his house. "Hey, it looks like my dad's home early from work," he said changing the subject.

Neither lizard said anything for the rest of the walk home. They both stopped in front of Iggy's house, and Liz gave him a hug. It wasn't one of those half hugs. It was more like a full on, I've been away on a long trip, two-arm, squeeze Iggy's back spikes, kinda hug.

"Let me know when you need help next time," Liz said as she pulled away from the hug.

"Um thanks. Have fun at the lake." Iggy felt his cheeks getting hot, so he fidgeted with his tail and turned around to breath. Liz was being super nice. Well, she was always nice but this time she was being like really *nice* nice. This sentimental stuff was freaking him out. Iggy decided he should stop wearing the cologne.

After walking inside, Iggy stopped in the entryway and dropped his backpack on the ground. He took a deep breath and noticed the house smelled funny, like saltwater. He figured his dad had probably brought out the beach supplies from the garage.

Just as Iggy was about to go up to his room, he

stopped on the first step and turned back around. For some reason, he suddenly got a strange feeling. "Mom?" Iggy asked. The word seemed to ring in his ear when no one answered. The house seemed awfully quiet. "Dad?" The same thing happened. "Molly?" Wait, she was at Little Bit's. He would have called Lily's name if she could answer.

Iggy walked through the living room and into the kitchen to see if his parents were in the backyard. That's when his heart almost jumped out of his chest. There on the ground, next to a *Hang Ten* backpack lay a blue visor.

8
A Turtle Holiday

Iggy couldn't stop staring down at the objects on the floor, like he had just found a one hundred dollar bill on the ground. "No way!" Iggy shouted. "No way!"

His eyes scanned the entire downstairs until the back door swung open, and there stood none other than Snap Shell himself wearing his Star's baseball cap and catcher's mitt. The turtle was standing straight up on his two flippers!

"Snap? What on earth are you doing here?" Iggy laughed and yelled at the same time.

"I'm going with you to Galveston tomorrow!" Snap said.

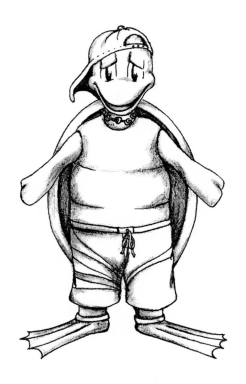

"You knew?"

"Yep. I've known for weeks. My pops called yours, and they made the arrangements for me to come down and go to the beach with you and Dragon D."

"Did you miss school today?" Iggy asked.

"Nope, it's a holiday. *Egg-lay Day*."

"Egg-lay Day? Is that like Labor Day?"

"Not quite, brah ... you know, for all the sea turtles.

The huge Egg Laying Festival is this weekend, but that's not really my thing."

"I can't believe you knew the whole time," Iggy said.

"I almost let it slip on the phone with you the other day," Snap said.

"So that's why you said *see ya soon*?" Iggy laughed and continued, "Hey the guys want to come too!"

"Sweet! I brought my board."

"You're going to surf?"

"Duh dude! I've never surfed in the Gulf before. Gotta add it to my list."

"Awesome!"

Iggy's parents walked inside. "You boys want to head out to the field like old times?" Mr. Green put a hand on both boys' shoulders.

"Of course we do!" Iggy yelled and grabbed his gear bag out of the closet by the back door.

Once they got to the field, Snap was already munchin' on a pack of sunflower seeds. The iguana and turtle assumed their normal positions out in the bullpen and started to warm up their arms.

"Boys! You've got the whole field. Why are you in the bullpen?" Mr. Green yelled.

"It's tradition Dad!" Iggy yelled back. Mr. Green waved them on and ran a few laps around the field.

"So how's school going man?" Snap said and spit out a seed shell.

"It's still the same," Iggy said and threw a fast one to the turtle.

"Yeah your mom told me about the whole study group drama. You've gotta watch out for a fly eater!" Snap spit out another shell.

"It was pretty bad."

"Hey, it looks like your arm's doing good though," Snap said, considering this was the first time he had thrown around the ball to his pitcher since Iggy had hurt his arm.

"Yeah. I'll be fine by tryouts next season."

"That's good brah. Too bad for Liz. She'll be back in the girls' softball league huh?" Snap laughed and continued, "What's up with you and Liz anyway?" He threw the ball directly into Iggy's mitt.

"You know. It's cool I guess. At first she was only hanging out with Isabella."

"Who? You didn't tell me about Isabella. What is she? A tropical bird or something?" Snap laughed and caught the ball.

"No. An iguana!" Iggy yelled from across the bullpen.

"No way! Is she cute?" Snap yelled back.

"Yeah, but she's really stuck up and she annoys me."

"One of those ... pretty on the outside but ugly on the inside? So is Liz in your study group then?" Snap asked.

"Study group? What study group? It fell apart remember ... but I think Liz wants to help me study on our own," Iggy said. "It feels weird though. She was getting all mushy and stuff after school today."

"Sweet!"

"It's not sweet!" Iggy said and started to blush.

After the boys had enough fresh air, and Mr. Green clocked enough time on his run, they all went home for dinner. Mrs. Green surprised them with take out from *The Green Bun*, which happened to be Snap's favorite.

That evening Snap checked the surf report for

Galveston. "Looks like the waves will be breaking in the morning."

"I'll call the guys!" Iggy made a phone call to each of their friends to let them know to meet at his house at eight o'clock in the morning, and Snap turned on the world news report.

Once Iggy got off the phone, he sat down in a beanbag next to Snap. "I didn't tell them you were coming."

"Good. We'll surprise them too."

"What are you watching?" Iggy asked.

"A bill's getting passed in the Senate."

"Really? That stuff still happens. I *just* made a note card about that."

Snap laughed. "Yeah, all that stuff in your social studies book is for real Ig."

"So new laws are still being made?" Iggy asked.

"All the time."

"Really?"

"Bills are always trying to get passed. It's not like every one of them becomes a law, but anyone can come up with an idea to start a bill. It has to get proposed to a legislator."

"Wow. Do you watch this channel all the time?"

"Dude. What do you expect ... I read the paper every morning too," Snap replied.

Iggy sat there with his eyes glued to the TV. He started to think about his last conversation with Cooper. Maybe there was a way to help Cooper appreciate social studies too.

◆　◆　◆

When Iggy woke up the next morning, he was so excited for the beach that he couldn't stay in bed a moment longer. He sat up and threw a pillow at his best friend's head, who was curled up in a giant sized sleeping bag.

"Duuude!"

"Morning sunshine!" Iggy said and jumped to the floor, barely missing the turtle's head.

"I never even heard the alarm go off!" Snap looked up at the clock and rubbed his eyes. "No wonder. It's only six o'clock man!"

Iggy pulled his curtains open to let the light in.

"Dude! Knock it off." Snap stuffed his head under his extra pillow.

"Come on Snap! It takes you *forever* to get up, so you might as well start," Iggy said, taking back the pillow to make his bed.

"That's because I'm not a morning animal man. Not to mention, it's only four in the morning where I'm from," Snap groaned.

A quarter past seven, Iggy heard the rev of a Mustang engine and ran downstairs to meet Dragon D. He hadn't seen his cousin since he left for college.

Dragon D burst through the door without ringing the bell. "What's for breakfast?" he asked immediately and gave Iggy a fist bump.

Snap walked downstairs in his *Rip Shell* board shorts to check out the commotion. "Yeah, I'm starving."

"Snap! What's up man? Walking on two I see." Dragon D gave Snap a big pat on the shell.

All the reptiles headed to the kitchen to see what was for breakfast.

Mrs. Green handed them each homemade fruit granola bars. "I want you all to be careful and stay with Dragon D," she said.

"They'll be fine!" The dragon gave his aunt a big hug. "Promise."

Mrs. Green kissed her nephew on the cheek and handed him a tube of sunscreen. "Make sure all the boys put some SPF on before you get out in the sun."

Snap Shell grabbed the tube from the dragon's hand. "I'll be needing that, thank you."

Mr. Green walked into the kitchen behind them. "There's our college lizard! How's school treating you?"

Dragon D gave his uncle a handshake then a hug.

"This semester's *way* better than the last one. All my classes start after lunchtime."

"No way! That would be awesome," Snap said.

Mrs. Green kept on with the motherly precautions. "Now you all know to pay attention to the flags out there. If they put up a red one, get out of the water." She looked directly at Iggy and Snap.

"But Mrs. Green, that's when the surf is the best," Snap joked.

Mrs. Green put her hands on her hips and gave the boys a narrowed eye look meaning, *no messing around*.

After a few more granola bars, Iggy and Snap helped Dragon D load their bags and gear into the trunk of his bright green convertible Mustang. They had to strap Snap's surfboard to the back.

Surfboard ✓

Boggie boards ✓

Towels ✓

Cooler ...

Snap glanced around. "I'll go get the cooler!" Snap said and walked back inside.

While Snap was inside, Cooper walked over from next door with Kit Kat, and Iggy introduced his friends to Dragon D.

"Sweet ride," Cooper said and nodded to the dragon.

The cat was the first to notice the surfboard strapped on the back of the trunk. "Do you surf?" Kit Kat asked Dragon D.

"Nah, that's Snap's board," Dragon D said.

Kit Kat gave Dragon D a puzzled look, and soon his mouth dropped open when he saw who turned the corner. "What? When? Snap?"

114

"No way!" Cooper yelled.

"Did you move back?" Kit Kat asked.

"Nah, dude. Just in town for the weekend ... turtle holiday," Snap said. "Nice bangs dude." Snap reached for Kit Kat's forehead.

"Hey, cut it out! Cat Clips messed it up and had to give me bangs." Kit Kat batted at the turtle's hand and smoothed his hair back.

Cooper spoke up. "Hey, you're walking on two feet like ..."

Snap cut him off, "Like you guys?"

"Well, yeah." Cooper shrugged.

All right guys, you can catch up on the drive. Let's ride!" Dragon D hopped over his seat and put his key in the ignition. The rest of the animals followed his moves and jumped in the car. Well, except Snap. There was no hopping over a car door when you're a box shell turtle.

"Wait. What about Buddy?" Cooper asked.

Iggy turned around from the front passenger seat, "Oh, he had to go with his grandpa to help out at some big ant farm. I talked to him last night," Iggy said.

"Old Mr. Horn, huh?" Snap laughed and scooted back in his seat.

"Ouch!" Kit Kat yelped.

"What?" Snap snorted.

"Your shell's taking up all the room."

"That's not my fault dude, there's no room back here," Snap tried to move over.

Iggy realized he should probably trade seats with Snap, so everyone got out and switched seats. Once the entire car was rearranged and Kit Kat was comfortable, the cat grabbed a popsicle out of the small cooler below his feet.

"Those are kinda for when we get hot ... you know?" Iggy nudged the cat and closed the cooler.

Kit Kat lifted up his arm to give Iggy a clear view of his armpit.

"Eww! Never mind. Have as many as you want." Iggy cringed.

Snap opened up the tube of lotion and gave it a squirt, sending a line of it straight into the backseat.

"Hey! Watch it!" Kit Kat meowed. "I don't need any of this stuff."

"Sorry man," Snap laughed and rubbed in a nice layer of white all over his bald head.

"Are you guys ready yet?" Dragon D said and reversed down the driveway.

"Not quite," Snap said and plugged his MP3 Player into the stereo and turned it to his beach cruisin' play list. "Now we're ready!" Snap said and turned his visor to the side. "Let's ride!"

9
Crazy Crabs

Iggy couldn't have asked for a better day with his friends, the sun on his scales, the wind in his face and Snap's surf songs in the background. This would be the life if Kit Kat's hair wasn't blowing in his mouth.

"I just swallowed your hair!" Iggy yelled to the cat.

"What? I can't hear you!" Kit Kat yelled against the wind.

"Your hair is down my throat!" Iggy yelled again.

"Why is your mouth open? Just cough it up?"

"I'm not a cat!" Iggy covered his face with his hand for most of the ride.

After a nice long drive in the wind, the bridge came

into sight. The boys perked up to get a better look at all the boats in the bay.

"What's that smell?" Kit Kat asked.

"Probably your arm pit," Cooper said.

Snap took in a deep breath, "Come on dude, it's saltwater," and turned around, "YIKES! What's up with your hair man?!"

Everyone turned to Kit Kat who looked like a fury tumble weed with whiskers. His hair was sticking out in all directions.

"What?" the cat asked.

"You may want to get in the water after all to tame your wild mane," Iggy said and pointed straight out ahead, "Look! There's the ocean."

Once they got to Seawall Boulevard, the scenery completely changed, and the beach came into view. The shore was crowded with all kinds of animals taking advantage of the nice weather. Little kids were jumping over waves and building sand castles with shovels and cups. Families were riding bikes, Segways and beach cruisers up and down the seawall.

"I want to ride in one of those," Cooper pointed to a family of ducks in a bright yellow cruiser, paddling as hard as their little flippers could manage.

"Looks like a lot of work to me," Kit Kat moaned. "Can't we just relax?"

Dragon D pulled into a parking spot near a huge sea turtle statue, and Snap opened his door before Dragon D had a chance to even turn off the engine.

"Hey, what's that all about?" Iggy got out of the backseat and pointed at the statue.

Snap spoke up. "It's the *Great Storm Statue*. They put it up a few years back after the 100th anniversary of the big hurricane that wiped all the turtles' houses away."

"Whoa! How'd you know that?" Cooper asked as he climbed out of the back.

"I used to live here brah," Snap grinned and looked around. "Pretty nice swells today." The waves were crashing hard to the west of the nearby pier. "Four footers," Snap said and directed Iggy's attention toward the pier. There were tents and tables with surf logos all over the beach.

"What's going on down there?" Iggy asked.

"Looks like a surf camp or something," Snap said while untying his board from the back of the car.

The rest of the animals grabbed their gear and walked down a set of concrete steps to get to the beach. They all unrolled their beach towels and plopped down in the sand, except Snap. He immediately started to wax his board.

"What are you doing that for?" Kit Kat asked as he dug for another popsicle in the cooler.

"Keeps my flippers from slipping all over the place dude." Snap kept on until the board had a nice layer of wax from nose to tail. "You guys wanna see a few tricks?" Snap looked up from his board with a grin.

"Go for it man!" Cooper waved him on.

"Don't have to tell me twice. Laters!" The turtle gave his friends the *hang ten* hand sign and ran off. Right before Snap got to the water's edge, he tied the leash to his ankle and headed out without looking back.

"What was that for?" Cooper looked at Iggy.

"It's a leash. It keeps him from losing his board when he falls off," Iggy explained.

"He must fall off a lot if he needs a leash," Kit Kat laughed.

"Not exactly," Iggy said. "Just watch."

Snap swam farther and farther out into the ocean. As the animals watched from the shoreline, Snap found the wave he wanted and got ready by laying on the belly of his shell. He hopped up and rode left from rail to rail and pumped up enough momentum to lift off and entertain the crowd with an air trick. *The superman.*

"Gosh! He's like ... good!" Cooper yelled, staring straight ahead. "He doesn't waste time either!"

"That's because he's got to take advantage of a good wave," Iggy said.

"Aren't they all pretty much the same?" Cooper asked.

"Nope. Not all the waves are going to be big enough to give him air like that. He's gotta be ready for the good ones," Iggy said.

"You sure do know a lot about surfing little cuz," Dragon D complimented.

Iggy nodded. "Yeah, I guess." He realized spending an entire day at Snap's competition in California taught him a thing or two about surfing. Maybe he didn't have a bad memory or a concentration problem after all. He never thought about it before, but maybe he just learned better through experience.

Snap rode a few more waves and ended with an *air reverse*, twirling his shell in the air on his board. His friends cheered.

Once Snap got back up to the beach, Cooper patted Snap on the shell. "That was cool man!"

"It was okay. The waves were starting to die down, so it was kinda hard to get air on that last one," Snap shrugged.

"It can't be that hard," Kit Kat said and stood up on top of his boogie board, pretending to surf in the sand.

"Please, let us see you try." Cooper hopped up on his own boogie board and started to do the same.

After a few more hours on the beach, lunch and a boogie board lesson from Snap, the animals were ready to ride some beach cruisers. Everyone headed back up to the seawall to put away all of the extra gear and towels in the car.

They walked across the street to Joe Crab's Rental Shop, which had bikes and cruisers in every color lined up in front of the shop. There was a sign plastered across the door with a picture of a huge king crab wearing a black eye patch like a pirate. Iggy assumed the crab must be Joe.

Dragon D opened the door for everyone, and the animals walked inside. The shop was dark and dingy, reeking of the musty smell of seaweed and of stale tuna. Iggy had to bat his way through a huge cobweb, which connected two sets of old rusty bike handles together. He felt like he had just walked into his Grandpa Green's attic. And if that wasn't bad enough, Joe Crab wasn't wearing his eye patch.

Snap was the first to notice. "Dude. Looks like he got in a fight."

Iggy shivered at the crab's empty eyeball socket.

"Crabs are known to fight for each other's shells, but usually hermit crabs," Snap whispered to Iggy.

"Why would he not cover that thing up?" Iggy whispered back to the turtle.

"Intimidation," Snap said and grinned.

When Kit Kat saw the missing eyeball, he squeaked out a meow.

"Was that you?" Cooper asked. "It sounded like a girl."

"I didn't hear anything," Kit Kat said and shrugged.

"Dude, that *was* you! You meowed like a girl," Snap confirmed.

"Shhhh. Look!" Trying to change the subject, Kit Kat pointed at the crab who had a hook attached to the end of his arm replacing his claw. "What is this place?"

The crab stared straight at Kit Kat and started scratching the inside of his eyeball socket with the end of his hook.

"Okay, that's messed up. I'm getting out of here." Kit Kat turned and bolted for the door.

"Not so fast fur ball!" Joe yelled from behind the counter.

Meow. Kit Kat slowly turned back around.

"What do you boys want to rent? I assume that's why you're here." The crab came out from behind his counter, walking sideways over to the group. That's when Iggy spotted a big old rat packing up boxes of what looked like crab shells in the back of the shop.

"You mean this isn't a haunted house?" Kit Kat said under his breath as he walked back to the group.

Dragon D walked up to meet the crab. "Yes sir. We need a beach cruiser for the five of us."

"You mean a double surrey?" The crab corrected him.

"Yeah, one of those," Dragon D said.

The crab sized up Dragon D and asked, "You over sixteen son?"

"Yeah, I just turned twenty," Dragon D said. "What do you need to see my license and registration?"

"Son, I don't care if you can drive ... or if you're a registered motor vehiclist. Just don't go running over anything ... like my wife! She's always wandering around on nice days like today."

Iggy laughed under his breath.

Joe looked at Iggy and snarled, "Did I say something funny? You can't miss her ... she wears *two* patches!"

Iggy gulped, and looked helplessly over at his cousin for back-up.

126

"Okay. We'll be cool." Dragon D reached for his wallet, but the crab stopped him.

"Hey, hey, hey ... whatcha grabbing for?" The crab raised his hook.

"Um. Just my wallet sir ... I have to pay don't I?"

"Yeah, you've gotta pay. Nothing's for free." The crab paused and puffed up his shell. "What are you, some kind of dragon or something?"

"Well yeah, kinda."

"It'll be ten dollars for an hour. Your hour will start in exactly sixty seconds. So hurry up and get out. I don't like guys like you ... dragons, bob cats, beasts ..."

Beast? Iggy looked around wondering who the crab was referring to, and assumed it had to be Kit Kat.

With that Dragon D gave the crab a ten-dollar bill in exchange for a key with the number three written on it. Everyone walked quickly to the door, but Kit Kat was moseying around by the vending machine.

"Hey! You forgot your fur ball!" Joe yelled.

Iggy grabbed the cat by the tail. "We've got snacks in the cooler!" he said and hurried to the door.

127

"And I thought the surf shops in California were weird," Snap said once Iggy and Kit Kat got outside.

"Yeah, rock-paper-scissors for whoever has to give the key back to him!" Iggy yelled.

Dragon D unlocked the chain on surrey number three, and Iggy took a seat next to his cousin.

"I get the very front!" Kit Kat yelled and plopped down into the seat that didn't have to pedal. Cooper and Snap sat in the back, but Snap's flippers couldn't even reach the pedals.

"Looks like I'll be freeloading with Kit Kat," Snap yelled up to Iggy. "You know I'd help if I could."

"I'm just here for a vacation, not a workout." Kit Kat kicked back and put his paws behind his head.

Once the animals crossed the street and got a good start down the seawall, Iggy spotted a seagull overhead. It kept eyeing Kit Kat who had grabbed another popsicle for the ride.

"Kit Kat, did you really need another one? You're making the birds follow us now," Iggy sighed.

Kit Kat turned around in his seat. "It's hot out here!

You try wearing a black fur coat." He turned back around to get comfortable again and looked down to find a surprise on his leg. "Yuck! What's that?"

"What is it?" Iggy yelled up to him.

"Looks like white out," Kit Kat yelled back, staring down at his hairy leg.

"Seagull poop!" Snap yelled from the very back, holding back a laugh.

"Gross!" Kit Kat tried to wipe his leg, but it got all in his hair. "YUCK! Get me off this ride!"

"But we just got started," Dragon D said.

"Get me off this ride!" Kit Kat insisted.

"Okay, okay. Stop crying." Dragon D laughed and the animals stopped pedaling. Kit Kat jumped off and ran straight for the ocean.

"That's the fastest I've ever seen that cat run in my life," Iggy laughed.

The reptiles watched Kit Kat go into the ocean, but only halfway, to clean his leg. When Kit Kat came out with a dry top half and a soaking wet bottom half, it looked like he was wearing a pair of tights.

"Don't say a word," Kit Kat said when he reached the crew. He took a seat, and the reptiles started pedaling again, trying to hold back tears of laughter.

"Nice look," Cooper finally yelled up to the front, not being able to contain himself. "I didn't know they sold skinny jeans at the beach."

Iggy turned around to give Cooper a high five for that one and took his hand off the steering.

"Watch out!" Kit Kat yelled.

Iggy turned forward just in time to dodge a snow crab crossing the street. "Was that Joe's wife?" He looked back over his shoulder at the crab he'd almost run over.

"We almost hit her!" Kit Kat said.

"Nah. I saw her," Dragon D reassured them.

"She really does have two eye patches!" Iggy pointed at the crab dodging oncoming traffic. "Nice save!" Iggy turned to his cousin. He could only imagine Joe Crab's good eyeball bulging out of its socket at the sight of his wife flattened like a pancake on the boardwalk.

The animals pedaled down to The Strand to buy a few items and grab an ice cream cone. Iggy found a tiny jar of sand from one of the shops and considered buying it for Liz since she couldn't come.

"What do you want to buy that for?" Kit Kat came up to Iggy with his paws full of trinkets. "Just go get some sand from the beach and put it in a cup."

"Yeah, you're right." Iggy put the little jar back. "Why would you want a fish in a hula skirt though?" Iggy pointed at the item in Kit Kat's paw.

"Why would you not?!" Kit Kat put his items on the counter.

"Hey guys, we only have fifteen minutes before our hour is up. Get your stuff and let's get out of here," Dragon D said and headed to the door.

Kit Kat finally came out of the shop with a bag of stuff.

"Come on man, we've been out here for hours!" Cooper yelled.

"Whatever! I had to go back for pop rocks," Kit Kat said while moseying over to his front seat.

The ride back was a total body workout for the reptiles. Dragon D, Cooper and Iggy pedaled as hard as they could to get back on time.

"Kit Kat, can't you trade spots with Snap and help us out?" Iggy yelled up to the cat.

"We're practically there. You guys are doing great," Kit Kat said.

The animals got back to Joe Crab's shop with less than a minute to spare. They parked the double surrey in spot three and got out to stretch.

Iggy had to peel his sweaty legs off the seat. "Okay, rock-paper-scissors. Winner goes inside," Iggy said.

"That sounds like losing to me," Cooper shouted.

"It's the only way it'll work with five of us," Iggy said.

The group put out their hands, and after three rounds, Iggy's paper won over Kit Kat's rock. So he basically lost.

"See ya! Tell Joe hi for me." The cat waved Iggy along.

Iggy sighed and opened up the door to find Joe inside polishing his hook. As Iggy tiptoed forward into the shop, the door slammed and he heard a lady scream. Iggy jumped and Joe immediately looked up. Iggy turned around to find a crab stuck in between the door. It was Joe's wife.

"What are *you* doing here?" The crab raised his hook and glared down from his counter.

"I came to return the key," Iggy said.

"Not you ... her!" Joe pointed. "I told you you're going to get hurt wandering around like that!" The crab came walking straight toward them, but sideways.

Iggy opened the door to let Joe's wife in and quickly dropped the key off on the counter. The lady crab started going on and on about how she was able to dodge a truck, a bus, a double surrey ... but not a dumb door ...

Joe cut her off and asked again, "What in crustacean's name are you doing here?"

Iggy started to head to the door to give them their privacy and get out of there.

"I'm talking to you lizard!"

"Me?" Iggy turned back around. "I told you I came to return your key."

"What were you doing with my key?" The crab yelled and charged sideways over to Iggy.

"Ahh. We went for a ride in the surrey thing for an hour. Remember?"

Joe stopped at Iggy's feet and raised his hook. "You messin' with my stuff boy?"

"What? No!"

"You best get out of here before I call the police!"

"Police?" Iggy darted out the door. He ran across the street to where Dragon D's car was parked. "Those crabs are crazy!" Iggy yelled, while jumping in the car, "Let's get out of here!"

10
Professor Iggy

Dragon D put on his seat belt and looked back at Iggy in his rearview mirror. "What happened?"

"I slammed Joe's wife in the door!"

"What did you do that for?" Dragon D asked.

"I didn't know she was there!"

"Um, it looks like we may want to leave. NOW!" Snap pointed across the street at Joe running sideways out of his shop waving his hook in the air.

"Let's go!" Iggy yelled. "I'm pretty sure Joe thinks we stole his cruiser."

"What? But we paid," Dragon D said and floored it out of there.

"I told you he went crazy!" Iggy yelled.

Everyone turned around and watched Joe's mouth moving with most likely *less than* pleasant words and phrases.

Once the crab was out of sight, the animals started discussing other matters ... like Halloween costumes, sports, and later the conversation turned to school.

"So who's your teacher this year?" Dragon D asked.

"Old Gruff," Iggy groaned.

"The goat? I had him one year at Memorial," Dragon D said.

"Really?" Iggy scooted forward in his seat, but his seat belt held him back.

"Yep! I had Mrs. Buff too. Those two have been there forever!"

"I know. Mr. Gruff is the worst!" Cooper yelled from the back.

"He's not so bad. He can be tough, but I remember he was one of my favorites," Dragon D said.

"*Can* be tough? He's made me re-do my homework every night!" Iggy exclaimed.

"Yeah and he gives homework in every subject," Cooper said.

Dragon D went on. "Mr. Gruff helped me come up with ways to study and concentrate."

"What? He helped you?" Iggy was shocked.

"Hey, isn't that what you're having trouble with Ig?" Snap asked.

"Yeah, I can't remember anything," Iggy said.

"Everything's so boring!" Cooper yelled again.

Dragon D looked in the rearview mirror at the lizards. "Believe me, I remember what it was like. I used to make up my own stories to go with everything I was learning. I think its called association ... you should try it. I was literally entertaining myself while coming up with ways to relate to what I was learning at the same time. I still do that in college."

"Seriously?" Iggy asked.

"Yeah, Mr. Gruff used to call me his creative thinker. I spent most of my lunch breaks in his room."

"You did? I'm going to have to spend lunch in his room next week for tutoring."

"Me too," Cooper said.

"Not me. I *aced* that last test," Kit Kat bragged.

"So how does that *sociation* thing work?" Iggy asked.

"It's A-ssociation. Let's say you're studying something like the Boston Tea Party."

Iggy cut him off. "They threw tea into the Boston Harbor!" Iggy said, excited to have known what his cousin was talking about.

"Is that all that happened though?" Dragon D questioned.

Iggy and Cooper both looked at each other with blank expressions.

Dragon D went on. "In the 1700s, Parliament was trying to pass a new law called the Tea Act, forcing the colonists to buy tea from only one company and pay taxes to Britain," Dragon D explained.

"So that's why they were mad?" Iggy asked.

"Yep."

"How do you still remember that?"

"Well, tea and tax both start with the letter T. When I think of British lizards, I think of a bunch of reptiles with

English accents and wigs sitting around in a mansion drinking tea and discussing ways to keep 'unruly' colonists from getting away with making money. It's all a mental picture for me. I picture everything in my head and make up silly stories."

"Cool," Cooper said. "I make up stories all the time."

"They call that lying," Kit Kat laughed.

"Me too! Just not about history and stuff," Iggy said.

"Well, it always helped me to talk about it out loud too," Dragon D said.

Iggy pulled forward in his seat again. "It's kinda like a game then!"

"Yep. Believe me, I had the same kind of problems as you guys. But I didn't really think of them as problems. It's more of a creative way of thinking. Not everyone gets it."

"I get it," Iggy said.

"Me too. I'm going to try it," Cooper said.

"See Ig, I told you there were other ways." Snap turned around in his seat and thumped Iggy on the head.

"Hey! I know. I just had to figure it out."

Before they knew it, Dragon D was already pulling into Kit Kat's driveway. The cat gathered all of his goodies and got out of the car.

"Hey, you dropped your fish thing," Iggy said and handed the toy to the cat.

"Whoops. Thanks man. See ya!" The cat tried to wave but dropped more of his trinkets on the walk up his driveway.

Once everyone got dropped off, Iggy, Snap and Dragon D went home and played Playbox 7, followed by a private song and dance performance by Molly. She decided to enter the school talent show and needed an audience to practice her number on. Iggy would never admit it, but she was actually pretty good.

After Dragon D left to go stay with his parents for the night, both boys went upstairs, and Snap showed Iggy his favorite surfing website and a picture that was taken of him for the paper. Snap would be leaving early in the morning, so Iggy tried to soak up all the time he could with his best friend. They talked and played games until neither of them could keep their eyes open.

Iggy and his dad took Snap to the airport the next morning. Mr. Green helped Snap check in with an attendant who walked him through security to get his shell scanned. Once he was clear, the turtle turned back one last time to wave at Iggy, and just like that, he was gone again.

Once they got back home, Iggy went upstairs to get ready for church. He stopped by his sister's room when he heard her talking in a loud voice. He thought she said something about the Gettysburg Address, which would be strange to hear coming out of Molly's mouth, so he thought he'd check it out. Her door was slightly cracked open, and she was standing with her back to the door. When Iggy peeked inside, he noticed that Molly had set up what looked like a classroom. She had lined up all of her baby dolls in rows, and each one had a sheet of paper in front of it. Her miniature chalkboard was set up on her bed, and she grabbed a stack of cards from off her table. That's when Iggy spotted his social studies book. Sure enough, Molly *had* mentioned the Gettysburg Address.

Iggy didn't say anything. He didn't want Molly to know he was watching. He also started to think that she *may* be on to something. Teaching stuffed animals and baby dolls that don't talk back ... that was exactly who Iggy needed to use his coaching, well teaching skills on. "What a great idea!" Iggy blurted out.

Molly spun around to the sound of her brother's voice. "Intruder!" Molly pointed at her brother. "Why are you eavesdropping on my lesson?"

Iggy froze. "I'm not. Why do you have my book?" He had to think quickly.

Molly looked at Iggy then at Tink, then back at Iggy. "Why do you hang out with lizards who eat *my* pets?"

"Cooper told you he was sorry," Iggy said and noticed Tink flying around frantically inside her cage. "Why is she flying around like that?"

Molly glared at Iggy. "Morning exercises. Duh!"

"Can I just have my book back?"

"Fine." Molly walked over to her bookshelf and pulled out a picture book instead. Iggy grabbed his social studies book from off her table and walked back to his room with a big smile on his face. Thanks to his sister, he had another idea on how to study.

During the reading at church, Iggy couldn't concentrate on anything but how to get hold of Molly's dolls without her noticing. He started to recall her Girl Scout and dance schedule in his head, realizing he had a chance to study with her dolls almost everyday for at least a whole hour. Thursdays were the only days that he would have to worry about. Not a good thing, considering tests always seemed to fall on Fridays. He'd figure it out.

That evening Mrs. Green offered to take Molly and Little Bit to see *The Last Ladybug* and asked Iggy, "Are you sure you don't want to go dear?"

"No, I need to do some homework." Iggy smiled at the thought of having Molly's room all to himself for the first time, which also made him feel slightly weird.

Mrs. Green handed Lily to her husband, and Molly came prancing downstairs dressed head to toe in red and black polka dots. Iggy walked upstairs to his bedroom window to watch his mom and the girls leave.

Once the coast was clear, he grabbed his history book and the note cards he had made throughout the week. It was time to put Snap's idea, Dragon D's idea, Mom's idea and Molly's idea all together.

Iggy entered Molly's pink, prissy bedroom and locked eyes with Tink. The dragonfly glared back. Now to decide who his lucky students would be. Iggy grabbed a pug in a pink ball gown, a dancing panda bear, a baby doll in a bonnet that looked like Lily, a lizard in a leotard, a lop-eared bunny, a unicorn with a diamond horn ... *What is this an all girls' school?* Iggy thought and looked around the room. That's when he spotted a frog dressed in a suit and crown sitting next to Tink's cage.

"Thanks, Tink. You don't mind do you?"

The dragonfly hit the inside of her plastic cage, clearly showing her disapproval.

"Oh, did I take away your prince?" Iggy laughed and looked around the room for more males to even out the girl to boy ratio. He wasn't having much luck and had to settle for a penguin that Molly had tried to turn into a girl by putting a wedding dress over his tuxedo.

"This is just wrong." Iggy ran to his bedroom to grab his Mr. Potato Head out of his closet. "There ya go. You can take a seat in front," Iggy said to the potato. Now that Iggy had a few boys amongst his classroom, he was ready to go.

He erased the flower that Molly had drawn on her chalkboard and looked at his class. Everyone stared straight ahead at him, except for the dancing panda that somehow got turned on and was spinning in circles by the window.

"Excuse me. It's time to begin." Iggy ran over to the bear to turn her off. "Please have a seat." He set her on the other side of the penguin.

"Welcome everyone. I'm glad you could make it." All of a sudden Iggy started to feel silly that he was talking to stuffed animals and laughed out loud.

He wrote his name on the board and imitating Mr. Gruff's deep voice he said, "You will call me Professor Iggy. Please raise your hands if you have any questions." He laughed again then reminded himself to concentrate. He grabbed his note cards and asked his first question to the class. "Can anyone tell me who wanted to tax the American colonists in order to pay back debts?" He looked around the room. "Anyone ... anyone? Yes, Princess Pug."

In a high-pitched voice, the pug, well Iggy, said, "Britain."

"Yes, exactly." He looked down at his card. "And can anyone tell me why British Parliament passed the Townshend Act in 1767? Anyone ... anyone? No one?"

Iggy explained that lawmakers in Britain felt the colonists should help pay back debt from the French and Indian War. When the colonists refused the Stamp Act, they used the bigger Townshend Act, which used a tariff to tax all kinds of British goods. Iggy said, "So to help you remember the Townshend Act, just remember that the small Stamp Act came first, and the big Townshend Act used a BIG tariff to tax everything in the town when the *small* little stamps didn't work."

Talking out loud helped Iggy understand and remember what he had read as he skimmed through his social studies book.

"So can anyone guess what the word boycott means?"
Iggy looked around the room. "Yes, Toad?"

"A fight!" The frog prince said, in Iggy's voice of
course.

"Exactly! They refused again!" Iggy said with
excitement. He paused for a moment as the light bulb
went off in his brain. "Now I get the Boston Massacre
and Tea Party," Iggy said out loud.

After a full hour of teaching his class, he made a few

notes and announced that tomorrow they would be studying science. The topic would be pollination. After putting all of Molly's stuffed animals back where they belonged, he came up with an idea to make up his own pop quiz with questions he thought Mr. Gruff would ask on a test. Excited, he left with his potato head and rushed to his own room.

11
No Time for Baseball

Mr. Gruff handed out a pop quiz first thing on Monday morning.

"Another quiz? When are we going to get a multiple choice one for once?" Cooper asked while standing next to the pencil sharpener.

"Please sit down Cooper. I'm going to have to tape you to your seat," Mr. Gruff said to the chameleon who slowly tried to change colors.

"Don't even try it mister." Mr. Gruff glared over his spectacles at the chameleon whose face turned as blue as the sky out the window behind him. "And where's your homework?"

"Um, a goat ate it?" Cooper grinned.

"That might be funny if you ever turned in homework *for* me to eat! Begin your quiz." Mr. Gruff shook his head and trotted back to his desk.

To Iggy's surprise, either the quiz seemed a little easier, or maybe the stuffed animals really did help. He wasn't the last to finish this time, and when he turned in his quiz to Mr. Gruff, the goat actually smiled at him. Iggy started to think about what his cousin had said about Mr. Gruff being one of his favorite teachers.

"Um, Mr. Gruff?" Iggy spoke up while standing at the goat's desk.

"Yes Iggy?" he said still looking down at his papers.

"You taught my cousin Dragon D once."

Mr. Gruff slowly lifted his head. "Dragon D?"

"Yeah, he's a water dragon."

"Oh, I remember him," Mr. Gruff said and continued, "I knew you reminded me of someone."

"I do?"

"Did he tell you he use to be a daydreamer too? " Mr. Gruff asked.

Iggy fidgeted with his hands. Every time Mr. Gruff called him a daydreamer, he felt like maybe the old goat could read his mind.

"So did he tell you?" Mr. Gruff asked again.

Iggy regained his thoughts. "Um, he told me he made up different ways to study."

"That's right, and we'll be doing those same techniques in tutoring today, so be ready," Mr. Gruff said.

"We will?" Iggy asked enthusiastically.

"Of course son. Just because a few of you learn differently than the rest of the class, doesn't mean I'm going to let you all get away with daydreaming and wandering around the material. That's just lazy!"

Iggy wanted to tell Mr. Gruff that he found a new way to study by teaching, but he wasn't sure how to explain who he was using as students. Instead he told Mr. Gruff that he was ready.

That afternoon Cooper, Samantha, Iggy and a few others brought their lunches and materials into Mr. Gruff's classroom for lunchtime tutoring. Mr. Gruff had everyone sit at the round table in the back of the classroom, and for the first time he allowed Cooper to stand.

Each student was given a card and asked to pick a partner. Iggy and Cooper paired up and received a card that said: *A Conversation between Abraham Lincoln and Jefferson Davis.* They were to act out what a conversation between the two historical figures would sound like, which required them to research both men. Luckily Iggy had already read up on these two leaders, so he used his own teaching techniques to explain the situation between the Union and Confederate States to Cooper.

Cooper was so eager to act out the conversation, he came up with a whole fictional scenario between the men. It started with them eating hamburgers at *The Green Bun.* Next came a food fight with Lincoln squirting mustard on Davis and Davis throwing his bun at Lincoln's face, yelling he will never join the Union.

The lizards were the first to volunteer, and they acted out the whole scene, receiving a standing ovation from Mr. Gruff and their classmates once they were finished.

Samantha must have been excited too, because her usual smell emerged. Iggy was used to it by now.

"That was fun!" Cooper bowed and coughed.

Mr. Gruff continued to pass out scenario cards until their lunch break was over. He ended the session with a few words. "See students, it requires a desire to learn in order for us to do the fun stuff and receive the good grade."

Iggy beamed because it totally made sense. For the first time, Mr. Gruff sounded like he really did know what he was talking about. Iggy realized that acting and teaching both had something in common too. They forced him to talk out loud, which helped him remember the lesson.

At the end of the day, Mr. Gruff gave Iggy's class permission slips for their field trip to Moody Gardens and explained, "Each of you will be divided into a group of four for the tropical rainforest project. You will collect data on your particular rainforest during our field trip. Everyone in the group will get the same grade, so no slacking off."

"Awesome," Iggy said. Finally they were doing some real hands on studying. Maybe the rest of the year *would* get better.

Mr. Gruff called out names in groups of four. Iggy's was the second group to be called. "Group Two. The South American Rainforest. Iggy, Sid, Marc and ... Isabella."

Oh, great. Isabella. Iggy cringed. *So much for things getting better*, he thought to himself.

Mr. Gruff told everyone to exchange phone numbers with each of their group members. Iggy wrote down his number and email address on separate sheets of paper for each of the animals in his group. Sid did the same.

Isabella handed everyone a business card. "My email, cell, bedroom phone and website are all on here."

"Website?" Iggy asked trying not to roll his eyes. Then he turned towards Marc's desk and realized it was empty. Marc wasn't in class, *again*.

"I need everyone back in their seats. I have one more announcement to make before you go home today. At the end of the week we will be getting a new student transfer from Mrs. Parrot's class across the hall." Mr.

Gruff paused and took a bite of the paper in his hand. "It seems like no one can keep their discipline problems under control," Mr. Gruff said under his breath and sighed. He continued on, "Digger Dog will be joining us. So no funny business."

"WHAT?!" Kit Kat blurted out. Every student in the class immediately stared at Kit Kat. The bell rang, and Iggy met all of his friends outside the lockers to try to calm the cat down.

"Digger Dog? Seriously? We can barely pass by each other in the lunch line, let alone be in the same class together!" Kit Kat meowed.

"I bet he got moved because of that fight with the bull dog in his class last week," Buddy said.

"And how are we going to make it on a school bus together for the field trip? With my luck he'll be in my group!"

Iggy knew he couldn't stick around for long if he wanted to get a head start with Molly's dolls, so he slipped away quietly while the others listened to Kit Kat go on and on about his problems.

As soon as Iggy got home he walked straight up to Molly's room to get an estimated time of her departure. He busted through her bedroom door. "Ummm, hey Molly. How was school today?" Iggy asked unnaturally.

"Haven't you heard of knocking? What if I was doing something secret and private?"

"Come on, you're six years old." Iggy smiled and tried not to come across as condescending. He needed to be on Molly's good side for a bit. "So, are you headed to Little Bit's house?"

"No," Molly said, walked over to sit down at her table and leisurely poured a cup of invisible tea.

"No? Why not?" Iggy asked surprised.

"Not that it's any of your business," Molly said while setting a few fake biscuits on the plate in front of her, "but she's sick."

"Oh. That's too bad." Iggy tried to sound sincere. Tink flew over Iggy's head and landed on Molly's shoulder. Molly lifted her cup to Tink's tiny mouth to give her a sip of imaginary tea. Iggy shook his head. *Did that just happen?*

"So, I guess you'll have to go to Girl Scouts by yourself then."

"I suppose. Why are you acting so strangely?" Molly and Tink both glared at Iggy.

"I'm not. I just wanted to know how my favorite sister is doing these days." Iggy tried to sound convincing.

"Me? Favorite? What about the egg?" Molly blotted her lip as if it were wet with tea.

"Oh, well I've known you longer than Lily."

"You mean the egg?" Molly corrected.

"Yes, I mean the egg. My bad."

"Who's cuter? Me or the egg?"

Iggy knew there was no point to keep going. "You!" With that he ran out the door and downstairs to get a snack.

"Hey Mom! Hey Lily! What time are you taking Molly to Girl Scouts?" Iggy practically shouted.

"In about an hour or so? How come?" his mom asked.

"Oh, just wondering ..." Iggy said and grabbed a granola bar from the pantry.

Mrs. Green gave Iggy a look and handed Lily to him to

give her arm a rest. Iggy sat down with his baby sister, but every time he tried to take a bite of his snack, Lily grabbed for it.

"Hey Lily, stop. Hold on," Iggy laughed. Lily demanded his attention, so he put her on his knee and bounced her around for a bit.

"Be careful honey. You know she's fragile," his mom said.

"She likes it!" Iggy replied. Lily chirped, screamed and giggled repetitively as Iggy bounced her up and down. She let out a high-pitched screech when Mr. Green came through the kitchen door. He had on his running shorts and smelled like wet grass and sweat.

"Where have you been running, Dad? In the fields?" Iggy snorted when his dad got close.

"Sure did Champ." Mr. Green said then kissed Lily on the top of her head.

"Honey, you have mud all over your back. Did you fall?" Mrs. Green asked.

"Me? Fall? No way. Obstacle course. Training got pretty dirty today." Mr. Green's next race was an obstacle course that not only included running, but biking, swimming and evidently rolling in mud.

"Hey Champ! Astros are on tonight. Want to watch after Lily goes to bed?"

Iggy thought about his limited amount of time in Molly's room. "I've really got to finish up some homework, but I'll come down for score reports."

"I'm impressed son. You really are buckling down on your grades aren't you?"

Iggy nodded.

As soon as Molly and his mom left, Iggy darted to his sister's room with his Mr. Potato Head. He lined everyone up in their normal spots and pulled out his science book to begin the lesson.

The class was going great. Not only did Iggy put together a superb lesson, but the whole class had obviously been studying, since every stuffed animal made an A+ on the pop quizzes he handed out. Just as Iggy was about to compliment the unicorn for her excellent explanation of photosynthesis, someone knocked on his sister's door. He froze. Was Molly already home? His dad? What would his dad say when he saw Iggy was *playing* with dolls? The door slowly opened, and it was worse than Iggy could ever imagine.

"Iggy? What are you ..."

"Liz? Why are you ..." They both spoke at the same time, staring at each other.

Liz broke the silence. "I came over to see if you wanted to study. Your dad said you were already in your room studying and to go on up."

"But I didn't even hear the doorbell!" Iggy blurted out.

"I knocked. I didn't want to wake up Lily."

Of course, Liz was always thinking ahead and being courteous.

"I didn't mean to snoop around, but when you weren't in your room, I tried here. I just didn't think you would be ..."

"I know ... playing with dolls. I'm not exactly playing with them. I'm teaching them. Well, kinda. Okay, okay. I'm playing school. It's my only hope to pass fifth grade. Please don't tell anyone."

Liz smiled. "Well, can I play too?"

"Really?"

Liz pointed at the potato in a cowboy hat. "Mr. Potato Head?"

"Yeah, Molly has so many girly animals and dolls, I had to bring my old spud to add a few dudes to the mix."

Liz laughed. "That makes sense. What are you teaching today?"

"Science," Iggy replied.

Iggy and Liz played teacher and assistant until every possible fact about pollination, flower parts, photosynthesis and nutrients was memorized.

After an hour had passed, Iggy said, "We only have a few minutes before Molly gets home. I've gotta put everything up before she finds me out."

"That means I'm the only one who knows your secret to making straight A's?" Liz asked.

"I wouldn't say A's quite yet, but basically, yes. You're the *only* one who knows. And you promised not to tell anyone!"

Liz held out her hand for a shake. "Promise." The two lizards stood there hand in hand. She smiled at him again, and Iggy noticed her starting to lean in, which made him drop her hand. She gave him a tight hug and Iggy held his breath.

"See you at school tomorrow," she said and walked out of the room.

"See ya." Iggy put the chalkboard back by Molly's closet and grabbed his potato. And just in time too. As soon as he left his sister's bedroom, he heard Molly's voice in the kitchen.

12
Rude Awakenings

Friday morning Iggy raced to school with Molly tagging behind.

"Why in fairy's name are we going so fast?" Molly huffed.

"Sorry Molly. I'm excited that's all."

"For?"

"Moody Gardens!"

"What? You're going to Moody Gardens?" Molly screeched.

"Yeah. You've heard of it?"

"Why of course. They have butterflies there. No fair! Tink needs a friend."

"I don't think you can take the butterflies home, Molly," Iggy laughed and patted Molly on the head.

"Hey, watch my spikes!" Molly batted at his hand then reached up to fix her spikes.

Once Iggy dropped off his sister, he quickly turned the corner and heard a loud bark coming from the direction of the fifth grade hall. *There's no barking allowed at school,* Iggy thought to himself. Next he heard a familiar meow and that's when he realized what today was.

"Kit Kat!" Iggy shouted and immediately sprinted down the fifth grade hall. As he zoomed by the classrooms, Principal Horn charged out of the office.

"Iggy! No running in the hall!"

Iggy slowed down to a jog.

"That's still considered running Iggy!" Mr. Horn yelled.

At that point Digger gave his loudest bark, and Kit Kat screeched like a mad cat.

"What's going on!" Mr. Horn started jogging too and grabbed his pants at the waist so they wouldn't fall off.

Iggy got to the open door, and Liz raced out of the

classroom to meet him. Kit Kat was standing on top of Mr. Gruff's desk throwing soda cans at Digger, who was being held back by Sid's tail wrapped around his back leg.

"What happened?" Iggy asked Liz.

"Kit Kat coughed up a hairball on Digger's seat when he left for the bathroom."

"What? Why?"

"Digger called him a name."

"Like what?"

"Kitty Cat."

"Oh gosh." Iggy bit his lip. "So did Digger sit …"

"Yep."

Iggy crinkled his nose. "Gross! I'd be mad too. Have you ever seen one of those things?"

"Not until today." Liz shivered and stuck out her tongue.

Mr. Horn huffed and puffed and pushed in between Iggy and Liz. "Quiet!!!"

Sid quickly untied himself from Digger's leg, and Kit Kat jumped down from the desk.

"Where is your teacher?" Principal Horn honked.

"Absent sir." Kit Kat yelled and saluted Principal Horn.

"Both of you. Come with me." The horned toad marched both animals down the hall toward his office.

"Is Mr. Gruff really absent?" Iggy asked as he walked inside the room.

"Beats me." Cooper curled his tail, excited to have seen a good fight.

"So what do we do now?" Iggy looked around the classroom and eventually at Mr. Gruff's empty desk as the tardy bell rang.

"What about the field trip?" Buddy said.

"What about our six-weeks test on Monday?" Isabella reminded the class.

"Yeah, we're supposed to review this morning before we leave," Iggy said.

"We could alwaysssss do sssssstudy groupssssss." Sid slid over to Iggy.

"Or Iggy could teach the class! He's great at teaching," Liz said. Iggy gave Liz a look.

"Since when? No offense man, but we didn't really get much done at your house," Cooper said with a shrug.

"Well, we've got to do something." Isabella put her hands on her hips and pursed her lips.

"Come on Iggy, give it one more try," Liz said and grabbed Iggy's arm.

Iggy looked down at Liz's little hand around his forearm and blushed. "Okay, I guess I can use my note cards."

"Thissssss should be good!" Sid said.

167

Everyone got in their desks, well everyone but Cooper, and Iggy walked up to the front of the room. The class stared at him. He gulped and looked over at Liz, who gave him a reassuring thumbs up.

Time to be creative, he thought and looked straight ahead, making eye contact with Marc. "Hey, you're back," Iggy said. Marc nodded, and Iggy imagined his Mr. Potato Head smiling back at him. He looked over at Buddy and imagined Molly's frog prince. Next he eyed Cooper and turned him into the dancing panda who always seemed to be by the window. Liz was the unicorn, Isabella was naturally Princess Pug and Samantha became the penguin.

"Much better," he said out loud and started at the beginning of unit one in science. After teaching everyone an easy way to remember the steps of photosynthesis, he started his own review game and called on the students for answers.

"Yes, Princess Pug." He pointed at Isabella.

"What did you call me?"

"Sorry, I meant Izzy!" Iggy could hear Liz giggle.

After a good twenty minutes, Mr. Gruff walked in with Kit Kat and Digger dog, both by their collars. Everyone froze, and Iggy went back to his seat.

"Both of you ... in a corner, NOW!"

Digger bowed his head and walked to the right corner.

"But I like that corner!" Kit Kat said on his way to the left corner. Mr. Gruff ignored him and told the class to line up as he scribbled on his clipboard and gnawed away on a pencil. Iggy's group was at the front of the line when they got a knock on the door.

"Iggy, open the door. That's our parent volunteer," Mr. Gruff ordered from across the room.

When Iggy opened the door, his baseball coach was on the other side. "Hey Coach Brown. I didn't know you were coming."

"Yep." Liz's dad gave Iggy a high five.

The class loaded onto the bus, and Mr. Gruff put Kit Kat and Digger in two separate seats directly in front of him. Iggy took a seat next to Marc. On the ride to Moody Gardens, he figured he would see what was going on with the little guy considering he had missed two more days of school that week. The words that came out of Marc's mouth weren't at all what Iggy was expecting to hear.

"My friend from the hospital died," Marc blurted out.

Iggy just sat there. He looked at the mouse's big brown eyes and saw the sadness behind them. He finally asked, "What was wrong with him?"

"Cancer," Marc whispered.

Iggy wasn't sure what to say. All he could think of was, "I'm sorry Marc. Were you guys good friends?"

"Yeah he was the funniest dog I ever knew," Marc sighed.

"He sounds cool. I wish I could have met him. What was his name?"

"Josh," Marc replied quietly.

Attempting to comfort Marc, Iggy forced a smile. He had so many questions he wanted to ask the mouse, like why he kept missing so much school, or if he was afraid to be sick again, or did he know Josh was going to die, but instead he stayed quiet.

The silence was broken when Sid slid his head in between Iggy and Marc's seats. "Sssssso. You guyssssss ready for our project?"

"Hey Sid," Iggy said.

"I heard that the animalssssss who work at the gardenssssss are localssssss from the different rainforessssssssts all over the world."

"Really?" Iggy turned to face Sid. He could hear Isabella from behind him complaining about Sid's rattle tickling her arm.

"Yessssss."

"I wonder if we'll see any chameleons," Cooper said and perked up from his seat across the row.

"Look, there's one right now directing traffic." Iggy pointed at a dark green lizard with two tall horns coming out of his nose and forehead. Everyone turned as the bus pulled up to the entrance of a glass pyramid.

"Awesome! He's a Jackson's Chameleon!" Cooper shouted.

The animals piled out of the bus and lined up in one of their teacher's famous single file lines. Mr. Gruff signaled for the traffic to stop as his class crossed the street. Once the class reached the front, they were greeted by two frogs, who both had their species name around their necks. *Weird*. Iggy had never thought he would one day have a job that would require him to wear *Green Iguana* on a necklace.

"Look Bud, it's your brother frog." Iggy pointed to the elderly looking Monkey Tree frog.

"You mean great-grandpa? What about that one?" Cooper pointed behind the check-in counter at an even older Poison Dart frog.

"Wow, I didn't even know these guys existed in my species!" Buddy walked up to the bright blue frog.

"Ticket please," the old frog croaked and then hiccupped.

"Are you really poisonous?" Buddy had to ask.

"Ticket please," the frog replied annoyed.

"Just give the guy your ticket." Kit Kat rolled his eyes and handed his to the frog.

Buddy did the same and whispered this time. "Are you?"

"Yes." The frog leaned down and his eyes bulged.

"Oh." Buddy backed up, but didn't leave and stayed next to Iggy.

"Ticket please." The frog snatched Iggy's ticket and ripped it in half. "Here. Now move along."

"Come on Bud. I'm sure we'll see more inside." Iggy and Buddy walked through a revolving glass door and into the tropical rainforest pyramid. Iggy looked up in awe. The ceiling was made of glass, and everywhere he looked he saw green. The whole place was lush and full of radiant colors. Monkeys swung from branches, butterflies flitted around from flower to flower, and insects danced around the enchanting plant-life as if the rainforest was their own playground. Iggy and Buddy met the rest of the class next to a huge Cannonball tree.

"Look at these!" Kit Kat reached up to grab one of the decorations hanging from the tree. But Mr. Gruff intercepted with a switch.

"Ouch!" Kit Kat licked his paw. "Where did that come from?"

"Now class. The African and South American Rainforest groups will check in with me. And the other two will be with Mr. Brown. We'll meet back here at this big tree."

"You mean the Cannonball Tree?" Kit Kat snickered.

"Yes, I'm very well aware of what this tree is called, Mr. Kat," Mr. Gruff said and continued, "I need you all to find five plants or flowers, five trees and five insects from your assigned area. Remember to take notes and a picture of each one. Follow the signs and no going off the path."

Isabella pulled out her expensive camera.

"Okay, any questions?" Mr. Gruff looked around and removed a can out of his shoulder bag.

Iggy's group got together and looked at the map to decide which path to take. In the midst of Isabella explaining the best route, Iggy felt a tap on his shoulder. He turned, and to his surprise it was Mr. Gruff. Iggy jumped. "Yes, sir?"

The goat pulled him away from the group for a moment. "Iggy, I need to ask you something."

"Me?" Iggy cringed. He assumed he was in trouble. "I didn't mean to disrupt the class. I was only leading the study game since we didn't have a teacher ..."

"Yes, thank you for taking care of that. You're a born leader, but that's not what I need to ask of you."

Iggy let out a breath. *Born leader?*

Mr. Gruff went on. "You get along okay with Marc, correct?"

"Um, yeah. We played summer ball together sir."

"Very well. Do you mind making sure he's doing okay today?" Mr. Gruff asked.

"What do you mean?"

"Just keep an eye on him. Can you do that?"

"Yes sir." Iggy was curious to know if Mr. Gruff knew about Marc's friend who passed away.

"Good. Now back to your group."

Iggy walked over to his group still unsure what his teacher knew about Marc. He followed the others down the South American path until a Palm Viper greeted them. Sid shook his rattle signaling, *hello,* and the snake slithered down into the *employees only* area. Once his four foot tail made it all the way across the path, the group kept going.

"Look, it's an Old Lady Palm." Iggy was the first to find a photo worthy tree. "Isabella, take a picture!"

"This is so boring," she said while snapping a few shots.

"Come on. Lighten up," Iggy said. "I thought you liked school stuff."

"I'd rather just take a test. We should all split up and get this over with. And look, Marc's still down by that ugly plant we left. Why is he walking so slow?"

"I'll go get him." Iggy walked over to Marc and noticed he was reading up on a medicinal plant. The first words on the sign said it was used to cure cancer. Marc sighed, and Iggy realized that the mouse looked a little pale.

The group continued taking pictures and notes on a few medicinal plants and a few more trees and flowers. The exhibit was full of all kinds of insects and every type of butterfly imaginable. Isabella took a picture of an Orange Julia, native to South America, for the project.

On their way to the Leaf Cutter Ant Exhibit, Marc had to sit down and take a break.

"Seriously? You two are slowing us down," Isabella said and turned back to Marc and Iggy.

Iggy rolled his eyes and looked at Marc. "Just ignore

her," he said. That's when he noticed Marc's facial hair was soaking wet. So did Isabella as she came up from behind him.

"Gross. What's wrong with him?" Isabella said and stepped away.

"Are you okay Marc? You don't look so good." Iggy knelt down to talk to the mouse.

"No. I don't feel good," Marc said weakly. Iggy looked down at Marc and noticed it was hard for him to even hold himself up.

"You never feel good." Isabella rolled her eyes.

"Leave him alone. Can't you see he's sick?" Iggy exclaimed.

"That's why I don't want to catch anything from him."

"You can't catch cancer Isabella!" Iggy shouted.

Isabella and Sid both froze and stared at Marc.

Iggy couldn't hold in his feelings any longer. "Why do you have to be so mean and obnoxious all the time? You know that's why no one likes you!" Iggy could usually put up with Isabella's bratty remarks, but for some reason not when it had to do with Marc.

Mr. Gruff came up to the animals. "What's going on?"

Isabella's face turned red as the palm viper, and she ran down the path.

"Isabella! I didn't mean to ..." Iggy yelled.

"Iggy?" Mr. Gruff asked.

"Marc doesn't feel good sir. I think it's hard for him to breath." Iggy helped Marc get up. He felt horrible for blurting out Marc's business, especially when he wasn't sure what was wrong with him.

"Clearly. Come with me son. I think you may need a wheelchair." Mr. Gruff took Marc by the arm. "Iggy, please go find Isabella. Sid and I will take Marc to the front."

Iggy could hear Isabella wailing dramatically in the distance. She was probably crying next to some poisonous bush. He would have much rather helped Mr. Gruff with Marc, but he really didn't have a choice. "Okay, sir," Iggy sighed and sauntered down the path.

13
Busted!

Iggy found Isabella in the no trespassing zone, under a Weeping Willow. *How appropriate.* Her mascara was running down her face, which made her look like a Halloween nightmare. *That's why you shouldn't wear so much makeup,* Iggy thought to himself.

"Hey. You don't have to cry." Iggy stood over her.

"Go away!"

Iggy wished he had a tissue to give her because her wet face was making him feel uncomfortable. "I didn't mean to yell at you. It's just, you don't know Marc like I do." Iggy paused wondering if he should tell Isabella more about what was going on with Marc.

He thought that maybe if she knew everyone's life was not easy and perfect, she would actually have some sympathy.

Isabella looked up at Iggy. Her tear stained face looked like she fell in a mud puddle. "Go away! I didn't know he has cancer."

"Had. Had cancer. I don't know if it will come back. But he does get sick a lot, so it's not easy for him to do everything as quickly as we do when he's having a bad day."

"I just didn't know that about him," she sniffled.

"Of course you didn't know. Hardly anyone knows. And I'd like to keep it that way." Iggy's voice deepened.

"I promise not to tell. I feel awful."

"Well most of the things you say make *everyone* feel awful," Iggy said. He wondered whether or not to go on, but then again, he figured Isabella should hear the truth so he continued. "You need to put yourself in other animals' shoes sometimes."

"What are you talking about?" Her tone got defensive.

Iggy hesitantly said, lowering his voice, "Well, I mean

here you are, this ..." Iggy paused looking for the right words. "You're this really pretty girl."

Isabella started to bat her soaking wet eyelashes.

Iggy shook his head and continued. "I mean you're probably like the prettiest girl at school."

"Really? Prettier than Liz?" She tried to smile.

Iggy bit his lip looking at the mess on her face. No one was prettier than Liz. "You both are pretty."

"But you said the prettiest!"

"Okay, okay. That's not the point." Iggy started to turn bright red. "Look. You may be pretty on the outside, but you brag about everything you have, and you insult other animals about what they say and do. That's just ugly."

"What?" Isabella started to stand up.

"I mean, no one cares that you have a personal servant, and you get to go on vacation all the time or that you carry those dumb expensive purses. Animals won't like you any less if you didn't have all of that stuff."

Isabella got quiet. She sat back down and wiped her face, but the tears started coming back again.

"What? What's wrong?" Iggy thought maybe he had been too harsh.

"It's just that ..." Isabella's tears turned into a fountain of black. Iggy *really* wished he had a tissue now. He handed her a leaf.

"Thanks. It's hard for me to make friends," she admitted.

"But why?"

"It's hard for me to be nice."

"Why?" Iggy asked again.

"Because no one is ever there for me. I mean, I have my nanny, but she's paid to take care of me. I don't have brothers or sisters. My parents are always traveling around the world. The only way I can make friends is to show off what I have so they'll like me."

"Isabella. If you were nice, all of us would like you. Even Liz."

"What, Liz doesn't like me?"

"Yes, she does, but she's tired of all the bragging too. Don't be a snob, and you'll have real friends."

"But what if I can't be nice? How do I start?"

"If you would listen to what others have to say instead of always having a negative remark or one upping them, then ..."

She cut him off. "One upping? What's that?"

"It's when you always try to out-do everyone. Like if someone said they went swimming last weekend, you'd say, oh my dad added on a huge water slide to my pool."

"How did you know he did that?" She perked up.

"I didn't. It was *just* an example."

"You're right. I was always afraid to be myself. No one has ever stood up to me like this."

"Well, when you're nice, you're not half bad," Iggy said and shrugged.

Isabella got up and gave Iggy a hug, and he cringed hoping not to get mascara on his cheek.

"Thank you," she said.

"Don't mention it," Iggy said, trying to remove himself from her grip.

Before Isabella released him, they both jumped to Liz's voice. "What are you guys doing over here? This is a no trespassing zone."

Iggy backed away from Isabella as fast as he could. "Nothing. We were just ... just looking around for plants," Iggy said awkwardly.

Liz eyed Isabella and continued, "We've been looking everywhere for you two! You both are about to miss lunch. Mr. Gruff has been eating chalk like a mad goat!"

"What about Marc?" Iggy asked quickly, to take the focus off him and Isabella.

"He's with the Moody Garden's medical animals. I think Mr. Mouse is on his way here to take him home."

"Really? Is he okay?"

"No one told us anything. We've been trying to find you guys," Liz said.

"Okay, then let's go," Iggy said hoping to get out of the discomfort of the situation.

The lizards walked quickly back to the Cannonball Tree to meet Mr. Gruff. After coming up with a rather lame excuse for why they were in a *no trespassing* area, Iggy's group spent the remainder of the afternoon looking for the last of their fifteen items for the project. Isabella followed Iggy around for the rest of the day, and literally wouldn't leave his side ... the bus ride wasn't any better.

"Iggy I saved you a seat!" Isabella said and tapped the seat next to her. Iggy met eyes with Liz who was sitting directly behind Isabella, in the seat next to Sid. He hesitantly sat down.

On the ride back to school, Isabella fell asleep on his shoulder as soon as they hit the freeway. Iggy tried to push her head back, but it was no use. He was certain she was awake the whole time considering he saw her eyes flicker shut when he looked over at her. He could only imagine what Liz was thinking, sitting directly behind them and all.

Isabella didn't wake up even when they got back to school and everyone had started to stand up.

"Isabella! Wake up!" Now Iggy *knew* she was faking.

Liz walked past them, and Iggy stood up, forcing Isabella to catch herself. When Iggy walked away, Cooper stepped in and handed Isabella her purse that had fallen to the ground. Iggy would give anything for Cooper to keep her occupied, which was exactly what he did as Iggy got inside to gather his things from his locker. As soon as the bell rang, and Mr. Gruff dismissed the class, Iggy bee-lined it straight to Miss Jay's room. He grabbed his sister and headed home before Liz or Isabella could stop him.

"Why are you in such a rush? I didn't even get to confirm my meeting with Little Bit tomorrow morning." Molly huffed as Iggy grabbed her by the hand.

"I'm sure she won't forget." Iggy even carried Molly's pink backpack so she would pick up the pace.

On the walk to his house, Iggy's thoughts changed back to Marc. He knew something was up, so once they got home, he went straight to his room to do his own research to find information on Leukemia. He learned that it was a cancer of the blood or bone marrow. Iggy read about the different treatments, then got to a section about bone marrow transplants. He remembered his dad saying something about that. It looked like a pretty big deal. He bookmarked a few pages to come back to after dinner. He was determined to figure out if Marc's cancer had come back, even if the mouse wouldn't tell him.

The next morning, Iggy continued his research as he waited *patiently* for Molly to go play with Little Bit. He had planned a Saturday study session in her room. He looked up from his laptop when he heard the clanking of jewelry and bells. Molly headed downstairs with her pink backpack, dressed in a princess outfit and jewels. Iggy shut down his laptop, gathered his classroom materials and raced to her room.

He had prepared an entire review game for his stuffed animal class for the big six-weeks test on Monday. It included sections on math, science, social studies and reading, but before he passed out the last test to the dancing panda, he froze, thinking he heard Molly's voice. Suddenly, he heard the familiar clanking sound of jewelry. He dropped his last test, ran into Molly's closet and slid the door shut. A shoe fell on his head. "Awww!"

Iggy heard Molly burst through the door. "What in fairy's name is going on in here?"

Iggy peeked through the door crack and watched Molly pick up her unicorn.

"How did you get out of your pen?" She picked up a test. "What is this?" Molly walked over to her penguin and yelled frantically. "Penelope? Where is your wedding dress?"

Iggy moved his foot and realized he had thrown the penguin's dress in the closet. Another shoe fell on his head. "Ouch!"

Molly's eyes darted to the closet. She ran over and slid the door open. Iggy closed his eyes.

"Intruder!" Molly screamed.

Iggy slowly opened one eye and walked out of the closet.

"What is this, some kind of sick joke?" She held up her penguin. "Why is she not wearing her dress?"

"Penelope is wearing a tuxedo. She's not a girl. I mean he's not."

"They're all girls! No boys allowed." Molly turned and glared at the Mr. Potato Head. "What is *he* doing here!?" Molly ran to Tink's cage. "Tink! How could you keep this from me?" The dragonfly flew around in circles and kept hitting her head on the glass.

"Molly calm down. I'm not hurting your stuffed animals. I'm just using ..."

Mr. and Mrs. Green came running into the room. They looked down at Iggy and back at Molly with looks of confusion.

"Iggy?" Mr. Green questioned.

"Dad. It's not what it looks like."

"Yes it is. Iggy was playing with *my* dolls in *my* room behind *my* back!"

"I wasn't playing with them exactly. I was playing school. I was teaching them. It helps me remember."

"Remember what?" Molly snarled.

"Everything in my books. It's the only way I can make good grades ... if I teach things that don't talk."

"So you're playing make believe that you're a teacher?" Molly giggled.

"No!" Iggy grabbed his potato head, stomped out of his sister's room and slammed the door to his bedroom. His test was on Monday, and even if Molly agreed to let him use her room and dolls, he was too embarrassed now.

Iggy picked up the phone. "Come on Snap. Answer." He paced back and forth with his ear to the phone.

"You have reached the Shell residence. We are not able to come to the ..." Iggy hung up on Mr. Shell's message.

He got out his practice tests and started taking them himself. He figured all he could do at this point was ... study. As long as he made a B on his test he would be happy, but he would prefer an A. Actually he would prefer a 100. He started to get frustrated with the questions on the test as they all ran together and didn't make any sense. All he could think about was his sister telling him he was playing with dolls. And her dumb bug buzzing around like a crazy fly. What was wrong with that thing anyway?

"Concentrate!" He yelled at the top of his lungs, which sent Mrs. Green running into his room.

"Mom, I'm just trying to study! That's all."

Mrs. Green sat on his bed, but didn't say anything.

"What Mom? What is it?"

She still stayed quiet.

"Mom aren't you going to say anything?" Iggy stood up.

"Sit down honey. You're upset. You need to do something else besides study right now."

"But I can't fail this test Mom. And I can't concentrate. And Molly is so annoying!"

"Son instead of studying for the next few hours, why don't you do something else? Draw. Write. Go outside. You like doing those things. Get your mind off everything, and then sit down to study later. Maybe even try something new, like write a silly story about what you're learning in class."

"Write a story about photosynthesis and pollination?" Iggy asked.

"Yes. Wouldn't that be fun?" Mrs. Green kissed Iggy on the top of his head and left the room.

Iggy sat in his room and stared out the window. It was a nice day, but what did it matter? When Iggy got bored of looking at the tree outside, he laid his head on his table. He decided he would stay there for the rest of the day. Iggy closed his eyes and soon heard a buzzing in his ear. "Tink!" Iggy shot up and looked around. "When I catch you!" Iggy stood up and he spotted a GIGANTIC bumblebee.

"How in the world did you get in here?"

The bee flew over to Iggy's windowsill and paced back and forth, then disappeared through a crack at the bottom of the window.

"So that's how you got in here." Iggy ripped out a sheet of paper from his notebook and stuffed it in the crack. "I'd like to see you try to get through that!"

Iggy sat back down and stared out his window again. The bee got him thinking about pollination. And the trees outside his window got him thinking about photosynthesis. Then he looked up at the cumulus clouds, and that's when he got an idea. He flipped to a blank page in his notebook and wrote: *Buzz the Bee and the Tree*. Obviously that dumb bee was on a mission to pollinate something the way he flew off so fast, and he had to know there weren't any flowers in Iggy's room. That's where the adventure would begin.

Iggy wrote Buzz's story for the rest of the afternoon, of course including additional secondary characters like Sarah the butterfly, Buzz's Type A girlfriend who was totally obsessed with becoming a lead pollinator.

Puff would be the angry villain cloud that kept following Buzz around, and Martin the Moth would be a perfect best friend for Buzz. He was kind of a downer and complained that he always smelled something weird, but it was nice to have company. All the bugs had after school jobs working together for this crazy hummingbird, who founded the Capital P Pollination Foundation back in the 70's.

Iggy was very satisfied with where this story was going, and he had the perfect conflict revolving around the weather. Iggy used his science book to inspire more ideas for the story, and by bedtime, Iggy had filled up ten pages in his notebook, only taking one break for dinner and to use the restroom. He would have kept going the next day after church, but his group came over to work on their rainforest project. He wasn't looking forward to seeing Isabella at his house again.

The group was down to three because Iggy hadn't heard from Marc. No one answered the phone at the Mouse residence when Iggy tried to call either, but he didn't mind picking up the slack for his friend.

Iggy organized the project board, Sid glued and Isabella wrote with markers. Iggy kept noticing Isabella staring at him while he organized. He really wished she would just act normal for a change.

Once the project was complete, they checked over their work to make sure they hadn't missed anything.

"Well guys it looks great to me!" Iggy high fived Isabella and tapped Sid's rattle with his fist.

"Yessssss. Nice penmanship Isssssssy!"

"Thanks Sid. We all did a great job." Isabella beamed at Iggy.

Iggy proposed they do a little study session for their test tomorrow. He thought he should take advantage of having a study group, even if they weren't stuffed animals.

"Great idea! I brought my flashcards." Isabella started digging through her purse.

"You use flashcards too?" Iggy asked.

"Always! I got the idea from you." She winked at him.

"Me three." Sid pulled out his flashcards.

The group studied for a full hour. Once it was time for everyone to go home, Iggy offered to keep the project at his house until they had to turn it in. Iggy walked them outside and Sid slid away, but Isabella stuck around. Iggy noticed she was acting strange, *again.* At some point she had managed to put on bright pink lipstick.

"Thanks for helping me," she said and batted her eyes.

"Um, sure. I mean we all worked together," Iggy said.

"No, not with the project silly."

"What are you talking about then?"

"You know, the talk at Moody Gardens."

Iggy started shuffling his foot in the grass, because she was making him feel uncomfortable. Isabella quickly hugged him, kissed him on the cheek and ran off.

"Yuck!" Iggy wiped the lipstick off his cheek and looked around to see if anyone had witnessed what she had done. He looked up at his sister's bedroom window to make sure she wasn't spying. To his surprise, the coast was clear.

14
Please Don't Eat This One

When Iggy got to school on Monday, there was a bag of dried banana chips on his desk with a good luck note cut in the shape of a heart from Isabella.

"Who's that from?" Liz called from behind Iggy.

"Me." Isabella grinned. Iggy gulped.

Mr. Gruff started passing out the test, and Iggy immediately scribbled down his name to begin once he got his copy. *Phew. Saved by a test.* When he looked down at question one he realized, for the first time all year, Mr. Gruff handed out a MULTIPLE CHOICE TEST!

"Today students you will thank me and yourselves

for all the hard work you did this six weeks. Now as you *bubble in* your answers, you will find my methods always work."

Iggy sure hoped Mr. Gruff was right. He was used to writing out the exact answer to every question, not deciding between four answers. As he started the science section, he reminded himself he knew everything there was to know about pollination and photosynthesis, so he took a deep breath and began.

"Good luck," Isabella whispered from behind him.

"Thanks." Iggy turned his head, but got right back to his test.

The test seemed like the easiest one he had taken all year. He knew the answers before he even read the multiple choices below each question. Mr. Gruff's hardcore methods may have truly helped him.

When Mr. Gruff gave the five-minute warning, Iggy had been finished for a while. He walked up to Mr. Gruff's desk, handed him the test and his pollination story.

"What's this?" Mr. Gruff grabbed the story.

"Something I wrote over the weekend to help me study."

Mr. Gruff grinned slightly and flipped through a few pages with his hoof.

"It's not homework though, so if you don't like it, please don't eat this one," Iggy said.

Mr. Gruff laughed. "Nice work, young lizard. You're *just* like your cousin." Mr. Gruff set the story in the homework tray.

"Seriously though. You won't eat it right? I kinda want to keep it after you're finished."

"I don't think I'll have to eat anymore of your work Iggy." Mr. Gruff adjusted his glasses and grabbed a red pen. Iggy grinned and walked back to his seat.

After all the tests were turned in, the class lined up for lunch ... Digger in the front, Kit Kat in the back. Those were their permanent spots for the week. Mr. Gruff announced he wouldn't be back that afternoon, but Mrs. Buff would have the graded tests for them at the end of the day.

Iggy sat in his usual seat at lunch next to Liz. He looked over at Marc's empty spot next to him, which Isabella took the liberty of occupying once she approached the table.

"How did you like the banana chips?" Isabella asked as she sat down.

"Oh, I'm saving them for later," Iggy said.

"Perfect. Since they *are* your favorite."

Liz spoke up. "How did you know banana chips were his favorite?"

"He told me." Isabella smirked.

"You did?" Liz looked at Iggy.

"No, I have no idea how she knew that." Iggy couldn't decide where to focus, so he looked at his three guy friends sitting across from him with three big identical grins on their faces.

"Here Iggy. You can have my carrot sticks since you don't have any vegetables in your lunch today." Liz handed Iggy her bag of carrots.

"Oh! I have some hummus that would taste so good with those!" Isabella handed Iggy a bowl of hummus.

"I don't even know what this stuff is." He pushed the bowl away.

"Chick peas," Isabella said.

"He doesn't even like chick peas!" Liz laughed. "You don't know anything about Iggy."

"This is awesome!" Kit Kat clapped his paws together.

Iggy had never seen Liz act so clingy. "Girls, I brought my lunch. I don't need extra food, but thank you." Iggy got up to go get a drink, and when he returned the arguing had reached a whole new level.

"Iggy. Who do you like better, me or Liz?" Isabella asked.

"What? How could you ask that?" Iggy didn't bother sitting back down and packed up his lunch to go stand by the wall and wait for Mrs. Buff. He had no idea how to deal with this situation.

The drama followed him outside at recess. Liz picked up a baseball and asked Iggy to play a game of catch. Iggy had a feeling she did this because everyone knew Isabella couldn't play baseball. She would probably kick the ball if asked to play.

In the middle of their throwing, Isabella walked up to Iggy and asked if he would like to play zombie freeze tag.

"Can't you see we're playing catch Isabella?" Liz asked as she rolled her eyes.

"Yes, I can see that you are playing with *my* boyfriend," Isabella replied with a glare.

"What?" Liz threw the ball.

"Iggy watch out!" Isabella yelled. Iggy caught the ball, and the entire playground went silent. Everyone held still. Iggy stopped breathing. The ball dropped.

"You were about to knock out my boyfriend!" Isabella yelled at the lizard.

Iggy looked at Liz. "She is *not* my girlfriend. I don't want a girlfriend. I just want to play baseball. Why can't we all just be friends?"

Liz stomped away, and Mrs. Buff blew the whistle. All the guys came up to Iggy. "What happened?"

"I don't know," Iggy sighed. "Girls are so moody!"

"You can have my carrot sticks," Kit Kat laughed.

"Cut it out," Iggy shook his head and walked away.

Back inside Iggy could feel the tension rising. Isabella refused to sit in the seat next to Liz and took Marc's empty chair. She didn't say a word for the rest of the day.

Right before the bell rang, Mrs. Buff handed back the tests. Iggy really hoped he had aced it, and he sat on the edge of his seat waiting for his grade. Mrs. Buff looked down at him with a big smile.

Sure enough, for the first time all year Iggy made an A+. He grinned and clinched his fists. Nothing could ruin his day now, not even the girls fighting over him. He started to picture himself walking hand in hand with both of them swinging his arms. *Gross!* He shook the image out of his head and quickly gathered his things from his locker. He couldn't wait to get home to tell his parents about his grade so he ran outside to find his sister.

As soon as Iggy walked out the school doors, he was surprised to see his dad standing outside. He wasn't expecting a ride home from school today.

"Hey Dad!" Iggy proudly handed his test to his dad.

"Way to go Champ!" Mr. Green high fived his son. "You did it!"

Iggy and his dad walked to the car. "What about Molly?" Iggy asked.

"Your mom is picking her up."

Iggy looked at his dad. "Then why are you ..." He stopped and noticed something strange about his dad's expression. "What's going on?"

"Please get in the car son," his father said somberly. Oh gosh, there was definitely something wrong. His dad's tone completely changed.

"What is it Dad?"

Mr. Green buckled his seat belt and said, "It's Marc."

"What? What about Marc? Is he okay?" Iggy almost jumped out of his seat belt.

"We don't know yet. The doctors ran tests this morning."

"What? He's in the hospital?"

"Yes, he's back in the hospital son."

"I knew it," Iggy sighed.

"He's not doing well. They are checking to see if ..."

Iggy cut him off. "If the cancer came back?"

Mr. Green paused and took in a deep breath. "They're afraid that it has."

"But what about remission?"

"It looks like Marc needs stronger treatment. I thought you would want to go and see him, so we're going over to the hospital."

"Right now?"

"Yes."

"What about a bone marrow transplant? I read about it!"

"Maybe son. They're trying to find donors."

Iggy kept replaying all the signs in his head as he

sat in silence the rest of the way. He knew Marc was sick ... the hats, his pale face and the field trip. He even wondered if his teacher knew the whole time too. If only there was something he could do for Marc.

When they walked inside the hospital, a gust of cold, sanitized air hit Iggy in the face. He shivered at the smell of disinfectant.

Once they got to the sixth floor and out of the elevator, Iggy and his dad checked in at the nurses' station. A nurse in bright green scrubs, that were covered with smiling sun faces, walked them to room 605A. Iggy couldn't help but look inside each of the rooms as they passed by. Some were empty and others were crowded with family members.

Once they got to the room at the end of the hall, the nurse led them inside. There was the little mouse with all kinds of tubes and things attached to his arm. Mr. Mouse was standing at the window, and Mrs. Mouse was in a chair with one of Marc's little brothers. Iggy remembered Marc telling him that he had a lot of siblings once.

Iggy walked up to the bed and put his hand on the rail. "Hi, Marc."

Marc looked at Iggy and mouthed the word *hi*, but nothing came out. Iggy looked up at his dad, and Mr. Green gave him a look of assurance, so Iggy kept talking. "We finished the science project for you. It looks really good."

Marc just smiled. Iggy looked around the room because he didn't know what else to say. The room made him sad. There was a lonely vase of purple and red flowers sitting on the table. He was trying to take it all in. He had never had a friend who was sick. Marc looked so little and weak. Iggy tried to make small talk, but he could tell Marc could barely keep his eyes open.

After about ten minutes, Mr. Green said, "We should let him rest son."

"Okay," Iggy said. "Bye Marc. I'll come back tomorrow. Maybe I can bring a book or something." Iggy opened up his backpack. At the time he wasn't sure why he brought it in, but now it seemed like the right idea. He grabbed his lucky baseball out of the bottom of the bag and set it on Marc's nightstand. "I caught this at an Astros' game. It's a good luck ball. You can have it."

Marc managed to muster up another smile.

"That was very nice of you Iggy," Mr. Mouse said and walked the iguanas out of the room.

"Any news?" Mr. Green asked Mr. Mouse once they were in the hall.

"None of our family's bone marrow was a match."

Iggy cut him off. He had an idea. "What if I put together a sign-up sheet at our school so we can find a match?" Iggy was determined to do whatever it would take to help his friend.

"That sounds like a great idea, but we may have already found an outside donor," Mr. Mouse said.

"Great! Is it someone you know?" Mr. Green asked.

"It's someone we all know. I can't disclose who it is until everything gets approved."

"Someone I know?" Iggy stared at Mr. Mouse's big brown eyes.

"Thank you for coming to see him. You have no idea how much that means to Marc." Mr. Mouse gave Iggy a hug.

Iggy and his dad slowly walked down the hall, and Iggy wondered who Mr. Mouse was talking about. In the distance he saw an old animal in a hospital gown being pushed in a wheelchair. As the chair got closer, he realized the old animal was a goat. Iggy squinted to get a clearer view. It was Mr. Gruff!

"Dad look! Mr. Gruff's here." Iggy pulled on his dad's arm. "But why?"

The goat's wheelchair stopped once it reached the two iguanas.

"Mr. Gruff, are you sick?" Iggy asked hesitantly.

"No Iggy, I'm not," Mr. Gruff said fatigued.

"But why are you in a wheelchair?"

"I gave bone marrow today." Mr. Gruff revealed, and the nurse continued to wheel him down the hall toward Marc's room. "See you in class next week Iggy," Mr. Gruff said and managed to get a few more words out. "I knew you could make an A on that test!"

Mr. Green looked down at Iggy. "See son. Maybe your ball really is good luck." Mr. Green put his arm around Iggy's shoulder and guided him down the hall.

Iggy stopped walking. In that moment he realized who the outside donor was for Marc. "Dad?"

"Yes, son?"

"Forget everything I said about Mr. Gruff."

Mr. Green nodded.

On the drive home Iggy stared out the window in deep thought. After seeing his friend he couldn't help but think about how silly all of his problems were. They sounded so small and trivial to him now. Liz and Isabella, Mr. Gruff's extra homework, the tests, Molly's dumb dolls, Snap living in another state ... none of those things seemed to matter as much as he watched the world go by while looking through the car window. Everything was going to be okay. School wasn't that bad after all. All Iggy could think about was the grateful look in Marc's eyes when he walked into the hospital room. He could tell it meant something to Marc that he came to see him. He was glad that he gave his lucky baseball to Marc. To Iggy it was now just a ball, but to Marc it was hope.

ABOUT THE AUTHOR

Melissa M. Williams has been writing stories since she was a little girl. Many of her stories were inspired by real life experiences with her reptile pets she owned while growing up in Houston, Texas. During graduate school for professional counseling, Melissa began substitute teaching for elementary grades in order to learn from experiences in the classroom. As an author and public speaker, Melissa discovered a new passion to work directly with creative kids and started the *I Write Publishing Contest*, offering opportunities for children to learn from her own background in the world of writing. Melissa spends the year speaking at schools and giving hands-on insight behind the writing and publishing process during her creative writing presentations. Melissa also hosts writing workshops, summer camps and book clubs for kids throughout the year. It is her goal that her creative writing programs will not only inspire children to use their imaginations, but also strengthen the self-esteem of our youth and make learning fun again.

For more information about Melissa's books and programs visit www.iggytheiguana.com and www.MelissaMwilliamsAuthor.com.

A NOTE FROM THE AUTHOR - THE REAL IGGY!

In third grade, I got my first pet for making the honor roll. I didn't care much for furry animals because I was fascinated with scaly and shelled creatures. My dad used to bring home huge field lizards in the summertime, and on the weekends, we would go out to the bayou to catch turtles. So it probably made sense that when we went to the pet store, I headed straight to the reptile section.

Iggy was the cutest iguana in the whole aquarium! I took him home and treated him as if he were a baby. Iggy had birthday parties, school lessons, a huge ensemble of shirts and ties that I had sewn myself, a miniature Jansport backpack, hats and the list goes on. By the time Iggy was two years old, he could sit up on his hind legs for his favorite treat, bananas, and he was even potty-trained! When Iggy outgrew his aquarium, the three-foot-long lizard lived on top of my bookshelf.

As a little girl, I loved to write. I had a huge imagination! I would write stories about Iggy and his best friend, Snap Shell. Throughout the years, I had many different iguanas, horned toads, and turtles as pets, and many of my pets are main characters in the Iggy the Iguana story. Some of my best memories, still to this day, were my adventures with Iggy. Now his memory will live on in the chapters of the Iggy the Iguana book.

SPECIAL THANKS

There are so many people I would like to thank who have inspired the writing of this third book in the series. First and foremost, I would like to thank my Lord and Savior for putting certain people, ideas and opportunities in my way and along this journey. Thank you to my loving and supportive family for recognizing and nurturing the creative spirit in my early childhood years. Thank you to the LongTale Publishing team for all of your hard work and talent, and most importantly your dedication till the very end: Kelley Stengele, Sharon Wyatt and Sue Kinane, I couldn't do what I get to do without each of you. I'm so thankful for my dear friends who became a part of my proofing and story development team: Esau Flores, Kellie Tharp, Allison Melkie and Bobby Ozuna, thank you for spending those long hours and late nights critically examining different aspects of this story. Thank you August Wiley and Rachel Sorensen and the student critique group at The School at St. George Place for allowing me to research the 5th grade school environment. Thank you to Jalani and Elia Adams for giving me so many ideas during our Saturday in the life of a 5th grader adventure. Thank you to Lauren Neuman for your clever idea to include a skunk in this story. Lastly I would like to thank all of the students who I've had the pleasure to teach or work with who have inspired a desire in me to bring out the creative brilliance in children. It's so important to nurture the different learning styles of our youth, who often encompass an incredible strength and energy.

PURCHASES & OTHER INFORMATION

ONLINE ORDERS:
To order other Iggy books and merchandise:
Visit www.iggytheiguana.com and follow the purchase link.

Iggy the Iguana books and Turtle Town books are also available online at BarnesandNoble.com and Amazon.com.

INFORMATION:
For information about author school visits, creative writing workshops and public speaking requests email melissa@longtalepublishing.com or visit her website: www.MelissaMWilliamsAuthor.com.

CPSIA information can be obtained at www.ICGtesting.com
Printed in the USA
LVOW06*0023240913

353787LV00004B/8/P